Yes, You Can

Yes, You Can

Dr. Ashutosh Karnatak

Ocean Books Pvt. Ltd.
ISO 9001:2015 Publishers

Published by
Ocean Books (P) Ltd.
4/19 Asaf Ali Road,
New Delhi-110 002 (INDIA)
e-mail: info@oceanbooks.in

ISBN 978-81-8430-260-8
Yes, You Can
by Dr. Ashutosh Karnatak

Edition
2023

Price
₹ 200.00 (Rupees Two Hundred only)

Printed at
Narula Printers, Delhi

"Mantra to Win the World"

Fight one more round.

When your arms are so tired that you can hardly lift your hands to come on guard, fight one more round.

When your nose is bleeding and your eyes are black and you are so tired that you wish your opponent would crack you one on the jaw and put you to sleep, fight one more round. Remembering that the man, who always fights one more round, is never whipped.

– James Corbett

Acknowledgements

The journey started on 27 September 1999 while I was taking my morning walk in Ajmer. As I looked around me and saw the diverse activities, the multifarious moods of the early risers, an idea dawned on me to share my many thoughts with the people. I decided to come out with a newsletter containing articles on positive attitude. I know of many write-ups that just preach, but I wanted to bring out something which can have positive impact on an individual. With the help of some colleagues, I started to bring out an inspirational newsletter and called it **"PLUS APPROACH".** The mission of the newsletter was to disseminate positive attitude, and act as a helping aid to the general masses, and I can say that I have been successful in this mission so far. In fact, I know of people who have changed their thinking pattern for the better after reading my articles. Even in my own house, my family members have changed their talking pattern to include terms like "Try Again", "Target", "Motivation" and "Focus".

This book is result of constant endeavor of more than four years. Seeing the success of my efforts with my newsletter, the idea struck me to put my thoughts and experiences into a book. The contents of this book relate to various aspects of our life. Most of the examples are from my personal experiences. Thus, I feel the readers will cherish the same and try to adopt them to improve their quality of life.

I am thankful to my readers who have encouraged and inspired me to continue with the newsletter. I am thankful to Dr. M. Akbar, professor IIM Lucknow, who inspired me by stating "Continue to spread positive thinking. There is nothing better than that...." I am thankful to my colleagues who interacted with me on various occasions on this subject. Last but not least I am grateful to my wife whose gave me quality time to enable me to accomplish my work in this direction, and my sons Tanay and Pranay who started using positive language in the house and in turn encouraged me to work in this direction. I am thankful to the publisher who has taken up the job of publishing the book, so as to make it available to all of you.

Plus - Plus

– Dr. Ashutosh Karnatak

Introduction

Life is a contract given by God and it is up to an individual whether he earns profit or loss from it. This book emphasizes on different areas to be honed so that one can lead a successful life and reap maximize profit. Humans have an inherent habit of blaming others or circumstances for their failures. To overcome this, the individual should analyze himself and make the necessary corrections in attitude and thinking process. If one is able to understand and amend oneself, he/she would be able to face the world more effectively.

The book, *Yes, You Can,* indicates that if a person develops plus or positive attitude in life then he/she can face any problem and situation. Success and failure are consequences of planning, strategy and action, and positive attitude is the result of mental orientation. In this book, emphasis is given to the role of the mind, and techniques to sharpen it. This book focuses on self-improvement, based on the premise that one should endeavor to control oneself, rather than try to change others. An improved self would be a better person, ready to face the challenges of the modern-day world.

Chapter 14 of this book deals with how one can deal with oneself. It has been observed that due to multidimensional work, man comes under undue stress which adversely affects his performance. This chapter on "Stress Management Techniques" lays emphasis on meditation techniques. It is observed that by practicing meditation, one's mind can be strengthened, which in turn would have a positive impact on the individual.

I strongly believe that if one's life is planned well, the results can be miraculous during the span of active life ranging from the age of 25 years to 60 years. The chapter on "Project Management Techniques" is meant exactly for this purpose. If the techniques mentioned in the chapter are used by the individual, one can reap good dividends in life without much effort.

I hope the readers will be able to develop and enrich their lives after reading this book. I also hope that the readers would the techniques to help others to develop positively by disseminating the "Plus Approach".

Plus - Plus

—Ashutosh Karnatak

Contents

1

Dreams

A human being is full of dreams. The dream to become someone special, someone different, to have everything he/she aspires for. A person after attaining adulthood aspires for admission in a good and reputed professional college. After graduation, he/she wants a suitable job that draws a handsome salary with good perks. Marriage is a natural part of the wish list. The list of aspirations for a suitable life partner can be very long. Good looks of the life partner, and being well placed both in the job and domestic fronts, are just a few of the dreams of an average youth who wants to marry. In good time, the person wants a child – a little son or daughter to add to the family. The wish list now gets bigger. A bungalow, a chauffeur driven luxury car, a good bank balance, are just some of the dreams of this average Indian. But this is not all. He wants recognition and fame and a fairly big bank balance – perhaps a crore rupees. A life spanning around 75 years, all-round prosperity and happiness, with grandchildren growing up and shaping into promising teenagers, form a great part of the individual's desires and dreams.

Though this is a typical dream list of an average person, not everyone manages to achieve all of them in this materialistic society. Achievements depend upon the mental attitude of the person, and how much he craves to achieve it. This craving is what drove industrialists like the Ambanis, Ruias or Late Gulshan Kumar to rise to such heights in society. They acquired whatever they wanted because they believed that they could do it. They are normal human beings like all of us, but with a difference in Attitude.

This book is an attempt in this direction. It is an endeavor to encompass various mental and other parameters that are essential, so to achieve success in life. In order to realize your dreams, go through the book not once, not twice...but till you feel a change in attitude and approach towards life.

❑

2

Attitude

"Life is a contract awarded by GOD to you. It is up to you, how you perform and gain out of it."

—Ashutosh Karnatak

Attitude of an Achiever

The dream narrated in Chapter 1 is generalized, which an ordinary person may or may not be able to achieve. But one can always strive to achieve it. While you are striving, you may encounter problems, hurdles and many obstacles. It is a proven fact that few people are able to successfully cross all such obstacles and hit the goal. The person who is able to do this is the Winner. This winner could be none other than You.

Have you ever tried to analyze the qualities of a winner? The one special quality in a winner is Attitude towards the work or the objective. This person too faces problems on the way. He/she too works with the same limited resources and parameters. But while this individual could cross over the bridge, you could not. It would be definitely wrong to say that you had not tried to achieve the goal, for you had surely put in the effort. But the blatant fact is, you did not win.

Fighting Spirit versus a Spirit to Win

The fighting spirit is what makes a person compete, but unless he/she has the spirit to win, the goal is just a dream. The winner gets a signal from his mind to go all out. This signal is on account of plus (+) or positive attitude. Edmond Hillary, who scaled Mount Everest, had plus attitude – the spirit to reach the peak. Classical dancer Sudha Chandran, lost a leg in an accident, but never gave up. Her positive (+) attitude made her continue with her dancing with an artificial limb. These are just a few examples of famous achievers to tell you that you too can dream and achieve whatever you desire. The only thing required is Plus (+) attitude.

What is Plus (+) Attitude

Plus attitude is a mental state of an individual, which is reflected in day-to-day activities. It makes one decide on objectives, plan strategies and achieve goals.

Major requirements for plus mental attitude are:

1. ***Clarity of Mind***

All the cobwebs of doubt and disbelief must be removed to achieve transparency of thoughts. All that you want to achieve must be crystal clear in your mind without any confusion. The goals for achievement may be according to the needs of the time, i.e. short-term or long-term. But clarity of thought and objectives are essential for reaching to any goal. This clarity of mind paves way to plus mental attitude.

2. *Desire to Achieve / Win*

"If a man has not discovered something that he will die for it, he is not fit to live."

—Martin Luther King Jr.

A person having a desire to achieve an objective can win the world without much problem. The reason is, he has the urge to succeed, or in other words, the Killer Instinct. Generally, people work with a half-hearted approach with no specific desire. With such an approach they may or may not achieve the results. When they do not achieve the results, they tend to leave the work half way and take up another job which seems more exciting at that moment. This happens because they are not ardently desirous. These are people who achieve average success.

All top successful people have the desire to win—the killer instinct. When you have strong determination, the hurdles on the way do not affect the final outcome. Rather, after crossing impediments the desire for achievement becomes stronger. Thomas Alva Edison invented the light bulb after carrying out around 10,000 experiments. He was so determined that after every failed experiment he would say that he had learned something to improve on future experiments. Such focus and desire to win is required to be a successful person, and this quality can be developed in a person.

3. *Try and Try Again*

This is the fundamental philosophy of achievers. They don't leave work half way through, whatsoever the difficulties or circumstances. A person with a plus mental attitude faces any adversity with courage, and in fact gets inspired to find a solution. Ultimately, the results are in his/her favor. It is worth noting that every unsuccessful attempt has the seed for successful results.

Never procrastinate. It is an age-old saying that any work in hand has to be finished the same day. So why not complete it and be a winner. Try and try again till the goal or target is reached. This also boosts your plus mental attitude.

"I don't believe in the word fate.
It is the refuse of every self confessed failure."

—Andrew Soutar

You, and only you, are responsible for your attitudes and the consequences due to it. It is common for a person to blame his/her failures on fate. Don't blame fate. It is not correct to make some third party responsible when you are unsuccessful. Have you analyzed the factors responsible for the failure? The percentage of fate in it could be hardly 10 per cent. What percentage do you attribute to your planning, resources or labour. We have often heard people saying: "Had my fate favored me, I could have achieved everything...." This fault-finding attitude is a sign of negative/minus thinking.

The ideal thing to do is to make a resolution to carve out your own destiny and your actions shall determine the same. In the epic Mahabharata, had Arjuna been fatalistic, he could not have fought the war against the Kaurvas. He realized that it was his *Karma* (duty) to do it. Once he had made his decision, his determination saw to it that he succeeded in his endeavour Therefore, resolve to do your *Karma* and assure a great future with plus attitude.

Plus Attitude and Active Life

Our active life is around 30 years,which is equivalent to 262,800 hours. If we work 12 hours a day, then your working life comes to 131,400 hours. Now in case there is minus attitude 50 per cent of the time, the plus active life is reduced to 65,700 hours, or half our active working life. So effectively the 30-year active life gets reduced to 15 years, or the active life time is shortened by half. However, if we improve our mental plus attitude to 75 per cent, the span of active life can be increased to 23 years. By further increasing plus attitude, substantial increase in active plus life can be achieved. It is worth noting that by adopting negative attitude, you not only reduce the active life, but also invite many ailments like blood pressure, stress and related diseases. So avoid anything negative. Develop plus attitude and lead a more active and positive life.

Signs of Plus Attitude

Ever smiling, unruffled with problems, a helping attitude, optimistic, courageous, generous, high goals and striving for that, these are some of the basic qualities of a plus-minded person. On the other hand, a person with minus or negative attitude would always have a frowning face, be disturbed, grumble, have quarrelsome or argumentative attitude, procrastinating tendencies and shirks responsibilities.

It is a fact that, by and large, people have a blend of both these qualities. But an individual who seeks to improve his negative traits can be termed as a plus-tilted person. This person, in course of time, cannot only realize a lot of improvement in his/her own personality, but the success graph would also show ascending tendencies. Such people want to improve and they are open-minded.

There are several people who do not like to listen to suggestions; in fact they dislike anyone trying to tell them they could be wrong. They are not ready to accept that they have any shortcomings. They always feel that their stand is correct, and the others are wrong. These people have a closed mind. They are people with minus attitude. Changing such individuals takes time. It requires a lot of effort. But if you have plus mental attitude, you can also change them.

Make this resolution daily:

I want to be identified as a Plus Attitude person.
I also want to strive to change the attitude of others so that they too have plus mental attitudes.

❑

3

Mind and Its Role

It is the mind that makes good or ill,
that makes wretch or happy, rich or poor.

— Edmond Spencer

Goals are achieved in life not just by dint of fate and labour. Mental attitude is a prime parameter that is required for the same. Right and proper mental attitude is desirous for achieving any sort of goal. Think for a while and visualize internal mental reaction. Now read further....

Mental Attitude and Success

Our attitudes shape our present and future. Forming a plus attitude towards a job is not difficult. But if you presume that a particular subject will not be completed, you can be assured this is exactly what will happen. This is not due to the fact that it cannot be done, but it is because of your negative mental attitude. Generally, our mind is conditioned before the work starts, and based on that we reap the results. Suppose we don't have an attitude to complete the work, the specific job is likely to suffer and remain incomplete. Therefore, the mind has to be conditioned to be in a positive state whatsoever the circumstances may be, and whenever it tends to go in a negative direction it should be pulled towards the positive side. Sending positive signals to the mind, as and when required, will definitely improve the success rate in day-to-day working.

There is a distinct relationship between mind and attitude. It has been seen that a person with plus attitude performs better than one with negative attitude. Let us now consider the relationship between mental attitude and performance. If we draw a curve between these parameters, it is found that performance increases with plus attitude and goes down with minus attitude. So, it is obvious that one should maintain one's attitude on the plus side. If it tends to tilt towards the negative, try and pull it back towards the plus side. Plus mental attitude can get you all the good things in life. It can help you overcome your difficulties and discover your strength. It can help you to step out ahead of your competitors. On the other hand, negative mental attitude is just as powerful, but instead of bringing in happiness and success, it can result in despair and defeat.

The choice is yours whether to have plus or negative mental attitude. But it will definitely help you if you sit quietly to contemplate, and rearrange your attitude towards the positive direction.

By now, it should be clear that success is a variable of mental attitude, and mental attitude is a function of the mind. Hence, it is essential to understand the theory of the mind and its intricacies.

Mind and Its Intricacies

We all know that the mind occupies a very small part of the total volume of the body. But, interestingly, it is this tiny part that directs our entire life.

All our actions depend on our state of mind. The actions of a person with plus attitude and another with a minus mental status of mind can be observed to be very varied and different.

Basically, the mind can be divided into two parts:

1. Active or conscious, or
2. Passive or subconscious

The active part of the mind plays a role in day-to-day actions, while the subconscious mind helps to shape our thinking pattern.

Our active mind is always busy thinking about something or other. It is always working and giving directions to us to take necessary actions. The subconscious mind, on the other hand, is a great storehouse in which much information is stored in an unstructured form, and continuously reacts depending on the circumstances. All such information is stacked like a heap of paper, without any order. So it is necessary to structure the information in the right manner, so that the power of the mind can be utilized to the optimum level.

Mental activity continues to exist in a passive mind, though we are not conscious of it. Though normally it remains dormant, our mind continues to store information and we can remember and retrieve it when needed. Interestingly, more unpleasant memories exist in a passive mind than pleasant ones.

The role of a subconscious mind can vary from individual to individual. You can understand it better if you contemplate and probe your subconscious and analyze its awareness level. Such introspection will lead to better realization of your subconscious/passive mind and its functioning.

Going deeper into the theory of subconscious, let us see the effect of subconscious mind while sleeping. You might be aware of a silent talk inside our mind while dreaming. You can listen to it vividly. This activity occurs in the subconscious part of the mind. In fact, during sleep, a learning process goes on, and the acquired knowledge is stored in the active/conscious mind. You must have observed that if you regularly get up at a specified time in the morning, it becomes your habit and you effortlessly wake up at that particular time every day. A message is stored in the subconscious mind regarding this, and at the specified time, it gives a wake-up signal to the conscious mind.

Formatting the Subconscious Mind

It is imperative to sharpen the capabilities of the subconscious mind, by practice or observation. The subconscious part is like a hard disk, and just as you would do for a computer, it will have to be formatted for use. As we know, all computer files have a particular location for storage and in case there are too many files in the memory, the speed slows down. Then, in order to set it right, the unnecessary and redundant files are removed from the memory, thus relieving the load on the hard disk.

Similarly, we have to program our subconscious for optimum utilization of the mind. All the information will have to be stored in a structured manner. This will lead to clarity of mind, which is essential for developing plus attitude and shall be helpful in achieving goals.

Potential of Subconscious Mind

In case you are insensitive to your subconscious, it will not be possible to achieve the required results. The subconscious/passive mind never sleeps. Its efficiency depends on your interest and aptitude. If it is not properly and fully used, the possibility of developing positive attitude is bleak. It is very essential to attain synchronization of conscious and subconscious mind. This is because the subconscious mind can act only when the conscious part permits it to do so. Hence, it is very important to tap the potential of the subconscious mind to the maximum extent.

Attack the negative thoughts and convert the active/conscious mind to positive attitude. Also sharpen the capabilities of the subconscious mind.

So, decide to control your mind, and be firm on this resolution.

Sharpening the Subconscious Mind

Formula 1

Condition your subconscious mind never to go towards the negative side. Whenever you feel ingress of negative thoughts, take control of your mind and virtually stop it from influencing you. When your active mind plunges into darkness, the back-up of positive thoughts from your subconscious mind flows in to enlighten your conscious mind. You have powers which you have never realized you had. You must stop thinking that you cannot do something. Think positive and say "I can do it". It can be done by formula 2.

"Do what you can, with what you have, and where you are."

—Theodore Roosevelt

Formula 2

In case you are depressed and feel you may fall into a negative cycle, send a suggestion from your subconscious mind to help overcome the negativity. This helps you to get back to the positive area of the curve. This technique is called self-suggestion or auto-suggestion. By practicing this technique, one can direct the subconscious mind to do any particular action. It is worth mentioning here that there is only a fine hairline difference between the positive and negative states of mind, and conscious endeavor should be made by you to keep yourself in the positive region.

If a negative signal disturbs you while you are engaged in some activity, it can be corrected by sending a feedback from the conscious mind to the subconscious part. If the subconscious mind acts positively, the results are in your favor. Otherwise, contrary results could be obtained.

Formula 3

Feed plus thoughts to the mind the same way as we recite or chant our prayers or mantra. This would help to maintain the subconscious mind in a plus state. It is necessary to repeat such thoughts as often as you can. For best results, schedule it for the morning and evening.

Formula 4

In order to meet the day-to-day requirement of life, it is essential to calibrate your mind with reference to the ideal mind of a successful person. This helps you find out where you need improvement. This could perhaps be done on half of yearly basis.

Some plus thoughts are as under:

- ***I will only think positive thoughts and not negative,*** because I have the power to do whatever I want to do.

- If someone hurts me, it may be due to his mental state at that moment. I must forgive him. That is, ***I must develop the attitude to forgive.***
- It is difficult to control the action of others. ***I cannot change an individual's attitude.*** It is his personality. He is master of his attitudes.
- On the other hand, ***let me control my attitude and myself.*** I can control my emotions and actions as I, and only I, am in charge of my emotions, thoughts and actions.

These formulae will have to be regularly repeated by the mind. It can be done while you are walking, taking rest, or any other time.

Conclusion

Attitude, efforts and actions help to shape positive frame of subconscious/passive mind. So, send positive signals to your mind and try to keep it in a plus/positive frame so that you can achieve the desired goals.

❑

4

Self-Renewal

Self-renewal may be a new term, but in this dynamic world, it may help you lead a successful life. It has been always impressed that whenever improvement is needed, never shy away. If self-renewal is necessary, then go for it. In the Bhagavad Gita, Lord Krishna sermonizes to Arjuna who is confused and perplexed in the middle of the battlefield. Arjuna was worried how he could even think of killing his kith and kin. At that juncture, Krishna explains to Arjuna how life is immortal and after death man takes a new form as if changing clothes. This is basically renewal of life. But if in the current life, one wants to renew him/herself, it can be done. It is basically a change in your outlook.

Some of steps towards self-renewal are as under:

1. Identify Your Potential

Most people spend their life without realizing their potential. However, if you want to be successful, this is a basic requirement. Identify the potential in yourself to excel in your field of expertise. It is necessary to start the exercise early in your childhood, but it is better late than never.

Every individual is different and possesses different capabilities. Hidden potential has been depicted by many people during explorations and experiments. Let us, for example, take the field of telecommunications. We are seeing so many new inventions and modernization taking place in this field, and everything is the brainchild of some individual or the other. Are they different from us? No, we too can excel. But we must find our potential.

Vast untapped sources of energy exist in every one of us. Many of us feel tremendous surge of confidence and energy during some part of our life. We feel charged for some time, but after a period many of us tend to lose interest. However, let us not generalize. Some of us do retain that internal charged and self-renewal state. We start behaving as a changed person-always charged, dynamic and more productive.

Think coolly about the concept and visualize yourself in the changed conditions.

2. Maintain Enthusiasm

Whenever there is a setback, we tend to feel depressed. We find fault or blame others for the turn of events. Such activity is a waste of time, as nothing fruitful would come out of it. We should rather face the adversity and bounce back. This can be done by exposing oneself to enthusiasm.

No person who is enthusiastic about his work has anything to fear from life. All the opportunities in the world are waiting to be grasped by people who love what they are doing. Enthusiasm keeps one always in an upbeat mood and it breeds emotions as well as mental chain reactions. Enthusiasm is like a spark which kindles fire inside and one can experience an avalanche type of phenomenon. Moreover, it is contagious. Associates of an enthusiastic person also tend to become excited about the job.

3. Remember Victories

All of us have passed through moments of victory at one stage or the other. The feeling emanating out of it should be stored in the mind properly. These happy thoughts come in handy whenever we pass through a bad phase. They help to divert you from the immediate depression, and pamper you with some self-kindness. This would reduce the feeling of guilt and inferiority that blocks the flow of power from the unconscious. It will help to bring happiness and self-esteem, and above all, energy back into you. This is self-renewal.

When you get up in the morning, feel like a new person who has also succeeded at a number of occasions. It is really a matter of inner feeling, as if freshly charged blood has stared flowing into your veins. Self-renewal is done by meeting challenges with full vigor.

4. Accept Challenges

When you meet a challenge, something in you will respond. This leads to self-renewal. But a lot of people don't find this so simple, because mentally they don't accept the challenge. They are afraid they will do something wrong and fear what people would say if the results are below par.

Do not be afraid of results. As it is said in the Bhagavad Gita—Do your *Karma,* Do not worry about results. In fact here, *Karma* means that you have to perform with full energy. Focus on the target with the belief that you are going to achieve great results. The outcome will follow automatically.

It has been seen that after failure, if you sustain for some time and doesn't break down, certain strong signals emanate from your brain to different parts of the body and the mind gets recharged. If you bounce back and accept the challenge, you are definitely going to win—this is the point of self-renewal. Find something that needs to be done and start doing it.

"Be desperate for results, inner desperation rekindles fire in the belly."

—Ashutosh Karnatak

5. Love Yourself

The key to self-development is to love oneself. You must have often heard sermons and philosophies asking one to love others, but is rarely taught or told to love yourself. Introspect yourself. Try to recollect how much you spend for yourself from your earnings, how much time you take out for yourself. The key is, if you exist, everything else that exists around you is an important part of your life. They relate to you. So love yourself and see the positive results that emanate.

"Courage is not absence of fear, but rather the judgement that something else is more important than one's fear."

—Ambrose Redmom

❑

5

Be Passionate

Very few people can openly admit that they are passionate. Most shy from giving an affirmative reply to whether they are passionate. After reading this chapter you will know why admitting you are a person full of passion will give you solace.

Here's an example. Tulsidas, the great Indian contemporary poet and author of *Ramcharitmanas* desired to have name and fame after he completed his great work. Despite being a devotee of Lord Rama, he could not keep himself away from such trivial desires. He went to his colleague Todarmal and asked him to convene a gathering wherein his work on Rama's story could be described. He felt this would fetch him fame. But even as the meeting was going on, he realized his fallacy. Having worked his whole heart on the great epic story, he felt he had done it for fame and not for devotion towards Lord Rama. He realized something was lacking in his worship, and that is Passion. Tulsidas described this feeling as under:

Kamihi Nari Piari jimi lobhihi priya jimi das;
Timi Raghunath Nirantar Priya Lagahu Mohi Ram.

(Hey! God, my love for you must be like passionate love to a woman and a greedy person's craving for money.)

Here the word Passionate describes the intensity of love of Tulsidas to God. In the same way, you should be passionate to the objectives/goals you wanted to achieve.

In the book *Lessons Form Top 20 Leaders of the World,* the authors Thomas J. Neff and James M. Citrin say that the common characteristic of all the leaders was their passion for the goals they want to achieve.... They love what they do.

"Having a passion for what you do, a sense of mission that comes from the heart, gives you energy, drive and enthusiasm that's contagious and essential for leading an organization."

—Elizabeth Dole

Bill Gates says "I have most fun job in this world, and love coming to work each day. There are always new challenges, new opportunities and new things to learn. If you enjoy your job this much, you never burn out."

Some advice to the young generation by leaders:

"Passion is probably the most important thing," says Daimler Chrysler's Bob Eaton. "I tell young adults, you have to be excited about going to work and trying to have an impact."

David Johnson of Campbell Soup says "Go out and do what you want to do. Don't wait and don't look for approval. And don't sit around wondering what will happen next. Push the pedal to the metal and make the most of life. Life is not a dress rehearsal. This is our life. This day is dying—Tick, tick, tick. What are you doing to make the most of it?"

This means kindling the fire inside oneself so as to be to reach the goal. Most people lack the will to do so, but whoever overcomes the lethargy, comes out a winner. Having moderate willpower may not be enough for achieving the goal. Albert Einstein had a passion for physics and spent many hours on solving problems, and Mozart had a passion for music. Both reached maximum heights in their chosen fields.

"One must have (PA-PP-PM) – Positive Attitude, Positive Passion and Positive Militancy to be a winner."

– Ashutosh Karnatak

Positive passion is essential, as explained above. It is like passion of an individual for the opposite sex, or the passion of a greedy man for money. If you visualize the mental frame of these two individuals, you can see only pictures of their object of passion hankering in their mind. They cannot think of anything else other than their objective. Even if they get digressed due to other subjects, it would only for a short while. Their thoughts always return to their main objective. Whatever they do it is for their objective. Whatever they think it is for their aim, their ultimate goal.

Similarly, winners must align and concentrate their energies towards their goal. It is a sure formula for success. There would be times when you feel disturbed due to one reason or another. At such a stage, try and converge your thoughts towards your goal. No force on this earth can stop such a person from achieving the set goals.

All this is easier said than done. But this does not mean it cannot be done. Follow the steps below and see the positive results for yourself.

1. Change the Thinking Process

Rather than blaming others or circumstances, try and introspect yourself and bring the required changes. This is the most important thing to do. Our mind is the main center of all activities. So, whenever our mind goes out of track, try to bring it back on the rails.

2. Supplement Passion by Militancy

Just having the passion for something is often insufficient to achieve one's goal. An extra ingredient is needed—militancy or fighting spirit to achieve. There is a very thin hairline difference between an aggressive mind and a militant one. While the first can be destructive, the second quality can lead to positive results. A man having no militancy in his mind may not able to rise up the ladder of success. He may stop well below the pinnacle.

Always feed auto-suggestion to your mind, "I can do it. It has to be done. I will achieve it". Whenever you achieve a target or any goal, celebrate it so that it becomes a remembrance. When you strive for another goal, recollect that occasion of winning or achieving. It will motivate you to achieve the new target.

Meditating on the target would also be helpful in changing the thinking process. In fact, the need is Belief. "Yes, I can do it". These are only five words but they are very powerful. While meditating, chant the same like a mantra. It is a proven fact that after some time you will find a change in your belief system.

Successful persons know that they can do it. They may not have been very brilliant at the beginning of their career, but with Positive Attitude (PA), Positive Passion (PP) and Positive Militancy (PM), they achieved their goal successfully. If they can do it, why not you! The answer is—Be passionate. It should be like a fire in your belly.

"Never speak of yourself to others; make them talk about themselves instead: therein lies the whole art of pleasing."

—J.E. de Goncourt

"The sages do not consider that making no mistakes is a blessing. They believe, rather, that the great virtue of man lies in his ability to correct his mistakes and continually make a new man of himself."

—Wang Yang-Ming

❑

6

Believe in Yourself

"I always knew I was going to be rich.
I don't think I ever doubted it for a minute."

—Warren Buffett 1930
(American Investment Entrepreneur)

Faith or belief is not new to mankind. Call it religion, philosophy, faith or by any other name, it varies from person to person, from community to community. But this has existed from time immemorial.

Let us take for example the belief of a person on who his parents are. It is a fact that, in this case, a person would have to totally trust and believe what he/she has heard from others. A child grows up believing what he hears and what he is taught. There is no instrument to check this other than a DNA test. But the belief is so strong, that no one challenges the fact.

Let's take another example. Many people strongly believe that whatsoever happens is pre-destined. This is not peculiar only to our country. This belief exists all over the world not only in old Greek mythology, but even in modern times. But such strong faith is very essential for any belief.

The above examples are given to explain that belief and faith are strong instruments, which if understood properly may help bring in tremendous success.

Faith is an inner voice. Trust your inner voice—it may well be the voice of wisdom. It is up to a person how to use it. Faith is also a matter of intelligence. It is a matter of instinct. It is planted inside every healthy human being. Just as a healthy bird rests on trees by instinct, just as healthy fish swim in water, so too the healthy human being is inclined to have faith and belief that enables him to swim across the sea of life.

A point to ponder, however, is that our faith does not remain steady. It often becomes shaky when we slip from our positive and faith-producing environment. It is at these times that we should resurrect the instinct of faith in whatever we do or follow. We must have total belief or faith in everything concerning ourselves—may it be on religion, self or what we do.

Strong belief is essential for a successful life. From the history of successful persons, it may be noted that they all had strong belief systems.

1. Belief in Religion/God/Supernatural Power

If a survey is done on belief in religion, round 80 per cent of the respondents will shall answer "partially yes and partially no". This indicates a deviation from total belief. It indicates that faith as a concept is not related to intelligence. It is something dealt by the subconscious mind and largely depends on one's upbringing.

When my children were young I asked them to offer water to the sun every morning. I told them that since the sun gives light to the world, we must be thankful to it. By giving it an offering, they would also derive energy from it. My children started following what I told them. Now after some time it has become a habit. They have started believing that by offering water to the sun they get power from it, and they could feel its effect.

Belief in God has existed from time immemorial. People of the Indus Valley Civilization believed in god of fire, water, etc. They instinctively worshipped these, with a belief that these elements have more power than even fellow human beings. Partial belief is very dangerous. Turning to total belief is better than otherwise, as you will be able to harness your mental energies in a positive direction. To fight against the stream needs more energy than to swim with the current, as it would leave you exhausted and unable to do real constructive work required for progress in life.

(a) The first step in this direction is to convert the mental attitude from partial to full. When you realize this truth, you will feel a definite solace internally. This belief is inborn and is not a derivative of anything.

(b) The second step is to convert negative thoughts of non-belief to positive ones of belief. This will help to cleanse your mind of the thoughts which were hampering your belief system.

(c) The third step is the most important—to sustain and surrender to the belief system. Whatever religion you follow, surrender to it *in toto*. Blench out all the negative feelings you have towards others. Remove your worries, pray to your God to take them and do whatever is deemed fit.

Whatever sins you have committed in any form, surrender it to your belief system. This will have a cleansing effect on your subconscious mind, which was so far burdened by these negative thoughts. Try to visualize the whole process for a minute.

- Sit comfortably at a peaceful place.
- Visualize your mind and mental process.
- Imagine that negative thoughts are getting out of your mind and are being transmitted to the environment through the belief system.
- You are getting unburdened of particular negative thoughts.
- After a few days, again sit quietly and repeat the process.
- After a month you will find a change in your mental reaction, reflection and personality.
- You can judge the enhancement of your spiritual growth and conscious level by yourself. Through this exercise, worries, anxiety, pressures and frustration would flee from your mind and you would feel more comfortable. This revitalized energy can be diverted towards achieving other real life goals.

The scientific explanation for the belief system is that this whole universe is full of energy. When you transmit positive thoughts of belief into the environment, it gets synchronized with similar frequencies existing in the surroundings, and you get the best results. There are several religious Gurus spreading positive knowledge, and their mass followers who believe in their virtues try to get maximum benefit out of them in times of crisis.

Let us take the example of the saint guru Sai Baba who is worshipped by people of different castes and creed. What brings the people together is their strong belief system that helps them get relief after worship.

There is no harm in developing or maintaining belief in a supernatural power termed as God. Different religions advocate different routes to reach this supernatural power. Staunch faith in God leads to clarity of heart and mind and helps in channelizing your energy in a positive direction to achieve the fullest results of your endeavors. God is an infinite energy source, and if the frequency of our mental attitude synchronizes with it, then maximum power can be derived. Many people have a low degree of faith, simply because they are scared to stick to the concept of a supernatural power or God. Let us not debate too much on the existence of God – let all agree that it is so, and let us surrender to it.

2. Belief in Prayers

Whether it is the Christians at Church, Hindus at temples, Muslim at the mosque or the sikhs at the gurudwara, all of them have their system of prayers as per their religious guidelines. The basic fundamentals behind prayers are the same for all devotees. They are all in search of some positive energy which will give them confidence. They surrender themselves to the superpower/God with their prayers. They chant mantra, go to temple or visit astrologers. With the passage of time, there are positive results and they feel happier. This is nothing but the result of belief.

One has to have strong belief in the prayers they chant. This belief is similar to the faith that a patient has on medicine given by a doctor. Most people consume medicines prescribed by their favorite doctor, irrespective of the fact that another doctor would have given theme the same medicines. But the treatment by the family physician is not only through medicines but it is also supplemented with positive thoughts and emotional treatment.

3. Belief in Oneself

Last but not least, believe in yourself. This belief is most essential for you to lead a successful life.

"In the presence of hope – faith is born;
In the presence of faith, love becomes a possibility;
In the presence of love, miracles happen."

The impact of faith is evident in the above quote,. "I can do it" is a sentence with just four words, but can have a large impact on your life. This message when chanted like a mantra sends positive signals to your mind, and your actions are regulated accordingly. On the contrary, questioning your capability is in itself a negative belief. It suppresses the power of your actions and the results are not commensurate to the efforts. So it is correct to say the man develops his belief system in life gradually, only after experiencing different events.

Sometimes failures shake your faith and belief. Try to analyze the cause of the same, instead of condemning the belief system. More composure is needed during this period. Generally, success feeds success and generates more success, which in turn strengthens your belief in yourself.

It is also not correct to say that with a strong belief system you will always succeed. But it is a fact that you will bounce back immediately. For example, Abraham Lincoln lost the elections seven times. But he believed that he had the ability to succeed in the long term, and history is the witness to his success. Thomas Edison failed some ten thousand times before he attained success in inventing the fluorescent bulb. These are just two of hundreds of successful persons who succeeded due to their "belief on self".

Conclusively, it can be said that in order to have success in life, the following three things needs to be practiced. Apply these principles see the success for yourself.

- Belief in Super Natural Power or GOD
- Belief in Prayer
- Belief in Self.

"It is always easier to believe than to deny. Our minds are naturally affirmative."

—John Burroughs
1837-1921, American Naturalist

❑

7

Stay Focused

We live in a world of distractions and often find it difficult to keep our mind focused in one direction. Let me give you a small example. A mother was trying to teach her son, but complained that he was not attentive. She scolded him, saying that his mind was somewhere else. She told him to pay more attention to what she was saying.

This is the problem with most of us. When we do a job, our mind has several distractions from all quarters. Due to this we are not able to achieve accuracy or quality in our work. When a multitude of inputs traverse through our mind, it could disturb us and we may not be able to concentrate. Consequently, we get reprimanded for having lost focus on what we are doing.

> *"There is no higher and simpler law of strategy than that of keeping one's forces concentrated. In short the principle is: act with the utmost concentration."*
>
> **—Carl Von Clausewitz**

In management jargon, we are told to have focus on a subject so that it is completed within the stipulated time with desired quality. Focus is the term, which has been talked about from time immemorial. Here is a little story from the epic Mahabharata that talks of focus. Guru Dronacharya was holding an archery competition for his pupils. He hung a toy bird on a tree and asked all his pupils to view its reflection through an oil bath kept on the ground. One by one the pupils came forward. One boy said that he could see the reflection of the beautiful sky, while another boy saw the image of the bird on the tree. But when it was the turn of Arjuna, the young archer said he could see only the eye of the bird. Arjuna then focused on the reflection of the bird's eye and hit his target on the dot. The success of Arjuna was due to his Focused Approach.

Similarly in history, Napoleon Bonaparte knew the value of concentrating on the enemy's weakest spot. This was his secret of winning over his foes. Single mindedness of purpose, total concentration on the goal and use of these qualities over the opponents, will always see that the arrow finds its mark.

The great epic Bhagavad Gita also has several examples of this concept. The mind, body and speech need to be employed in unity to achieve any target. Lord Krishna said "Hey Arjuna! He who always and constantly thinks of me with undivided mind, to that Yogi always absorbed in Me. I am easily available" This means that if one is focused on the goal, it is easily achievable. Krishna further says "He whose mind remains unattached to sense-objects derives through meditations the satvic joy which dwells in the mind; then having completely identified himself through meditation with Brahma, that Yogi enjoys eternal bliss".

So it is clear that from Napoleon to the modern Yogi, all used focused approach in achieving their goals.

This gives rise to a question—How does one develop focused approach? Some techniques are as under:

1. Believe in Self

A simple scientific experiment taught in school is to point the focal point of convex lenses towards the sun. It is observed, that anything kept under the lenses at the focal point gets burnt. This is because maximum solar energy gets converged at that point. Similarly, if we focus on some goal, all our energy is likely to get concentrated for achievement of the same. This is the key to success.

So, concentrate your energies on your goal. But to achieve this you have to have belief on self—belief on "I Can Do It". Only with such regulated feelings can our internal energies be canalized in a singular direction. The output of self is maximum when the internal resistance is least and when maximum transfer of energy takes place from the mind towards the goal. This way the goal is bound to be achieved.

2. Feel the Success

Focus can be defined as Feel Of Constant Urge for Success. This urge is required for constantly rekindling the feel. When a job is completed as per requirement, the feel of the outcome always sensationalizes you. A student who gets admission into a college of his/her choice after passing out of school gets exhilarated with the outcome. The point is that, if the student remains focused in studies, it is not difficult to continue to achieve goals. Let's take the example is of a writer's feelings as his/her book is about to be published. The feeling of success even before the book is out, gets the author charged to proceed further, and one day the book is published, and the goal achieved. A mountain climber has only one goal in mind, that is, the top of the mountain. The climber does not see what is on either side, but moves forward with just one goal. Even snowy winds or landslides do not disturb the focus as his/her mind is always imbibed with the feel of success.

It is seen at workplaces that employees, whether they are engineers, managers or even filing clerks, find that their excellence becomes effortless whenever they apply focused approach to the work. This is because they constantly feel the oncoming success. All their emotions are harnessed optimally during work time to deliver the desired results.

3. Meditating with Open Eye

When one is focused, it is state of meditating with the eyes open, i.e. one feel the disturbance of the environment but is not bothered by it as the focus is on a target. So this is nothing but meditating with open eyes. In this state, the attention becomes so focused that the individual is only aware of a narrow range of perceptions related to the immediate task and loses track of time and space. It is a state of self-forgetfulness, even self-consciousness. The individual becomes ego-less and control over the ongoing work gets enhanced. The responses too are perfectly attuned to the changing demands of the task at hand. Performance is at its peak while one is focused. A focused person is not concerned with how he/she is doing, of thoughts of success or failure. The sheer pleasure of the act itself is what motivates the person.

4. Meditating on the Gland

The fact of life is that everything is controlled by the mind, and mind governs secretion of hormones from the glands which controls all our actions. The pituitary gland is located behind our brain and controls our actions. In order to have more focused approach, meditation can be done on the pituitary gland. This would regulate the hormones being secreted by the gland. Consequently, when one wants to focus on a task, the gland would secrete in a regulated manner as required. With this, enhanced performance can be experienced. Sharpening of the glands can be done on regular basis in order to achieve more focus.

5. Develop Concentration

This is a matter of habit. Whenever you do any work, try to concentrate only in that job, as if nothing else exists in and around you. Give an auto-suggestion to the mind that you have to complete this job within a certain time slot, with best of qualities. Whenever your attention gets diverted, bring it back to the focal point of the work, so that you can deliver/convert most of your energy towards the goal.

One must intentionally focus sharply on the task at hand. This needs a highly concentrated state of mind. It may take some time to learn to get focused, but once it is achieved, lock it. Then it takes on a force of its own, both offering relief from emotional turbulence and making the task effortless. It has been seen that people concentrate best when the immediate demands are greater then usual, and they are able to give more than normal. A focused state of mind is a state of bliss. It can be easily co-related with state of worship when one sits to pray to God, when man totally surrenders himself to the Almighty. Similarly, you have to totally surrender yourself to the task at hand. When you are in this state, all the concerned glands secrete optimally and there will be no internal resistance. By practicing this daily, your performance improves and you will suddenly realize that the quality and accuracy of your work is improving.

6. Focused Approach

The concept of getting focused must be clear to you by now. One other aspect that must be getting clearer is that, before attaining a steady state of focused approach, a gradient is necessary. This could be anxiety, fear, challenge or some other factor, which automatically aligns all the energy in one direction. But for this, one needs to have a calm and quiet mind instead of an agitated one. This is because the brain works less efficiently when it is fatigued or nervous. It is also seen that one is more focused in one's area of core competence, but get distracted in areas in which one is not so strong. Thus, identification of areas of core competence is necessary so that one can get focused on them. It is helpful in channeling emotions into more productive output.

7. Focus on Profession

There is a stage in life when it becomes essential to focus on profession, and excel in it. The most important thing is to identify the goal and once it is set correctly, direct all your energy towards it and get the desired results.

It is a fact of life that all parents want their child to excel in all fields but by the time he enters adulthood, he youngster becomes a jack-of-all-trades. To avoid this, it is very essential that right from childhood, areas need to be identified where one can excel. Towing this line could make you too into one of the most successful persons in India, like N.R. Narayan Murthy of Infosys; Subrato Roy of Sahara India; Sunil Mittal of Bharti Telecom, the Tatas or Birlas, Sachin Tendulkar or Amitabh Bachchan, among others.

Now it is time to sit quietly, analyze yourself and develop a focused approach. Try to "Stay Focused" on whatever you do for the rest of your life, and succeed like the greats of our country, if not the world.

> *"A life without purpose is a languid, drifting thing; Every day we ought to review our purpose, saying to ourselves: This day let me make a sound beginning, for what we have hitherto done is naught."*
>
> **–Thomas A. Kempis**

❑

8

Maintain the Struggle Within

The term Struggle is generally used for fighting against others. But in the present age, wherein cut-throat competition is prevalent and day-to-day life is getting more and more difficult, there is a constant need to maintain an internal struggle within oneself. This is the best weapon to fight against all odds and succeed in your endeavour.

Have you ever had a smooth ride through any undertaking? Most probably the answer is a big NO. We always find constraints and impediments in what we do.

We all know that if we allow these constraints to take control of us, our work will be left half-way, and the goal will not be achieved. It could have been circumstances which compelled you to leave the work half way. But if you could have overcome the odds and sustained the struggle within yourself, positive results would have been achieved.

"Maintain the light of struggle within you, let it not die – it's a force leading you to succeed."

– Ashutosh Karnatak

Once an astrologer read a person's palm and forecast that he would be facing tension. The person answered that this was no problem, as he needed tension to move ahead. He said this led him to progress, as his mental faculties would not be able to develop if there was nothing to counter. This answer, though strange, aptly fits the description of the struggle within self. Although "Struggle" is a negative word, it generates all positive things like success, confidence and self-esteem. A man who does not struggle is seldom able to achieve the goal in life. Every known personality from history, from Abraham Lincoln to Nelson Mandela, has faced adversities in life and come out of it successfully. This is because their internal struggle was alive and they rekindled it whenever it was required.

Take the case of a bird which flies in the sky. The internal force/struggle is translated from its body to the wings and the bird flies. If its wings are clipped, it would not be able to fly and would ultimately perish. Of course, the struggle inside our body is not such that it would give us the power to have buoyancy in the air, because nature does not intend us to do so. But it is clear that even the expected results cannot be achieved if the struggle within us is absent. A minimum level of struggle must be maintained inside every individual and it should not be taken as a negative trait.

"No Bird soars so High if he soars with his own wings."

—William Blake

Here are some techniques to make the inner struggle live.

1. Convert Negative Circumstances to Positive Ones

If you believe that you will find green pastures throughout your life, you are living in a world of illusion. If you make a survey and ask people about their experiences in life, each on would narrate stories of their struggles in life. If these struggles are taken in a negative sense, then one will succumb to the circumstances and will not be able to counter it, and ultimately end in failures. This is what marks the difference between a man of success and another of failures. So, mentally convert the negative circumstances into positive ones and meet the challenge head-on.

2. Auto-Suggestion

This is one of the tried techniques which could be utilized to overcome any circumstance. You have to instruct your mind to face the situation squarely, and it would lead you to success. This would help in developing a positive frame of mind even in negative circumstances.

3. Fire in the Belly

This is the foremost requirement to live in this world. We must not leave things till they are completed in spite of any trouble or constraints. Whenever you find yourself encompassed in negative circumstances and you have no desire to move further, recollect the following slogan by Jim Corbett, and while you murmur it silently in your mind, image the lines as if you are actually there.

> Fight one more round when your feet are so tired that you have to shuffle back to the center of the ring.
>
> Fight one more round when your arms are so tired that you can hardly lift your hand to come on ground.

> Fight one more round when your nose is bleeding and your eyes are black and you are so tired that you wish your opponent would crack you on the jaw and put you to sleep.
> Fight one more round, remembering that the man who always fights more and more rounds is never whipped.

This is the type of fire which is needed inside the belly to face the world and to maintain your existence.

4. Refer to Past Events

Often, remembering past events acts as a stimulant. Recollecting how you had behaved and handled a particular situation could help you correlate with the present circumstance and inspire you to fight out the problems. By recalling past events, a struggle develops within one self and the urge to succeed increases.

5. Positive Militancy

The urge or fire within oneself helps to develop positive militancy in man. This is very essential if a person wants to progress in life. Militancy in this regard is positive and it should be developed to be so. Make it a habit to take up a job in a positive militant way and have the attitude to complete it, even if there are many hurdles on the way.

> *"Aggression and struggle within self are necessary ingredients for success."*
>
> **– Ashutosh Karnatak**

Often, people tend to avoid tension and resort to meditative techniques and other stress management methods. One fine point needs to be explained here. These methods could cure you from stress, but they also kill the militancy and struggle inside you. I am not advocating that you should remain in a stressful condition just to keep the fire inside you alive. The fact is that, if you don't have passion inside you, then you must develop and feel it. It will give you push to get up and inspire you to progress. Without struggle a man is nothing but a living dead.

> *"Originality and the feeling of one's own dignity is achieved only through work and struggle."*
>
> **—Fyodor Dostoyerslay**

> *"The ultimate measure of a man is not where he stands in the moment of comfort and convenience, but where he stands at times of challenge and controversy."*
>
> **—Martin Luther King**

> *"The most important thing a father can do for his children is to love their mother."*
>
> **—Theodore Hesburgh** (*Readers Digest*

❑

9

How to Conduct Yourself

In this age of cut-throat competition, particularly for professionals, every day existence has become quite difficult. We have to struggle to maintain ourselves as per the standards of the surroundings, so that we are not looked down upon by those around us. This can easily be achieved if we consciously remember "How to conduct self".

Earlier there were less skilled people and less stress on quality of work. People too were not so aware of quality. But now the situation is different and most people want to excel beyond their own limitations. It has become a rat race of sorts, and if you want to advance, you must know how to conduct yourself. This involves two aspects – Communication and Knowledge.

I. COMMUNICATION

There are two types of communication:

–Verbal

(A) Speech (Sentences, Vocabulary)

(B) Telephone conversation

-Non-Verbal

(C) Dress
(D) Gestures
(E) Smile and Laughter
(F) Hair
(G) Shoes
(H) Walk

Let's briefly take a look at each aspect.

1. Verbal Communication

Verbal communication is a reflection of one's personality. This could be both face to face or through the telephone.

(A) Direct Speech

You may come across persons with a huge body, but very low voice pitch, personalities contrary to this also exist. Voice has a very important role in communication. Let's take the example of India's popular cine star Amitabh Bachchan who possesses not only a good personality but also a good voice.

(a) *Voice Modulation*

Just having a good voice is not sufficient. It has to be trained to modulate properly in order to be able to communicate the same meaning as in the text. This needs practice. One needs to know how to use the voice astutely.

(b) *Clarity in Speech*

This is the first and foremost aspect of communication. Speech needs to be clear without mingling of words. Often people tend to stammer and stop in between a speech when they get stuck. In case you have difficulty in speaking, you can use proper punctuation or pauses to your advantage.

(c) Subject of Speech

You must be very clear in the mind what you want to communicate. The subject of the speech must be clear. In case you get deviated from the main direction of speech, try to recollect and bring the talk back to the main subject.

(d) Sentences

Usage of short and clear sentences while conversing reflects the personality positively. Use sentences which are able to communicate properly. Long sentences may be good while writing, as one can read it again and again to make oneself clear. But small and proper sentences are appreciated while talking.

(e) Vocabulary

Often difficult words are used during a conversation just to impress others. Always remember that a conversation is meant for the other person, not for you. The other person must be able to understand what thoughts you are trying to convey during the conversation. So, use language and vocabulary that a general person having common knowledge can grasp. Otherwise, the conversation tends to get boring, and the listener would feel like terminating the interaction early. Use simple but necessary vocabulary and the language in which the opposite party feels comfortable.

(B) Telephonic Conversation

The world has become so mechanized nowadays that a large part of the work or flow of information is through telephone. This mode of communication has become part of our life. In fact, a good percentage of common public on the streets own cell phones and communicate through their mobile phones. In such a scenario, proper communication is very much the need of the hour.

It is essential to have proper knowledge of the subject being discussed. The reply has to be to the point. It is better, if important messages are repeated for better understanding. The telephone system nowadays is well advanced and the signals are clear most of the time. So, avoid using a loud voice or shouting into the phone. Ensuring that the other party has understood the subject is the key of telephonic conversations.

2. Non-Verbal Communication

(C) Dress

Dress plays an important role in communication. In fact, dress is the first thing by which a person is judged, because visual impact comes first, speech and other things follow subsequently. Dress is the real reflection of one's personality. No one would take the liberty of entering into loose talk with a well-dressed person. Dressing for the occasion is also necessary. While formal wear should be the norm in the office and at official get-togethers or meetings, you can shift over to informal wear when you are with family or friends. This choice of appropriate dress code is very important for impressing others and getting due respect.

(D) Gestures

Gestures can be used very effectively for non-verbal communication. In fact, adding gestures to your speech is such a strong means of communication, that words become lackluster without them. Eyes, brows, hands and arms can be used very effectively along with your voice modulation. However, take proper care while using gestures, as they can be sometimes misinterpreted or misunderstood due to custom or habits of a particular place.

(E) Smile and Laughter

It is said that a smile costs nothing, but gives a lot as it makes others happy, whereas a frowning face is despised by all. Thus, maintain a smile on your face. It helps to solve many problems. Laughter, however, should be used sparingly in a controlled manner only when required. While in the office thunderous laughter is not appreciated. So, in day-to-day life, it is necessary to understand the necessity of using smiles, laughter or normal facial expressions.

(F) Hair

Baldness may be a boon in comparison to those who are not able to maintain their hair. Hairstyle that suits the personality should be identified and accordingly maintained. Generally, short haircuts are in vogue for men. But some people try various styles, which sometimes turn out to be awkward. Women, of course, experiment more with their hair and short and long hairstyles are both in fashion. But, in order to have a charismatic personality, a proper hairstyle is very necessary. So do also take care of this aspect.

(G) Footwear

Footwear is one of the main areas which needs attention in your daily conduct. You must use footwear befitting your clothes. Selection of shoes may also be based on the occasion, that is, wear sports shoes for jogging not leather formals. Another important point is that shoes must be clean and shining as this reflects the personality of a person. Dirty shoes or torn laces indicate that the person is too casual and does not take the work or occasion seriously. Ladies must especially take care that if nail polish is applied, it should be maintained properly and should not be chipped, as it reflects on the personality of the person.

(H) Gait

Style of walking or gait also reflects on one's personality. Top executives of companies walk fast. This is true reflection of their mind which processes many things at a time. The speed of the mind is reflected through the speed of the gait.

One has to regulate the style of walking as per the occasion. For example, if you are with a lady and keep to your usual fast pace while walking, it would not be appreciated as the lady would not be able to keep pace with you. You have to regulate the speed as the occasion demands. Also take care to see that your shoulders are straight and not slanted to either side, or stooped forward. A proper gait reflects a confident being. So, you have to also have control of yourself while walking.

II. KNOWLEDGE

While external personality is indicated by dress and grooming, the internal personality of the individual is reflected by the knowledge within. A well-dressed man having little gray matter is a failure. In fact, internal personality has more impact than external appearances. Often people with frail bodies are able to impress people with their strong knowledge. Here are some tips on how to enhance knowledge.

- Reading newspaper's, articles regularly
- Reading good books
- Going through newsletters or magazines of one's functional area
- Attending lectures of eminent persons
- Interacting with people of knowledge
- Internet surfing.

Therefore, updating yourself with the latest happenings around is an important aspect in your preparation for proper conduct.

The above-mentioned points for improving yourself in your day-to-day conduct will have a definite impact on your image, both in the way you face society and in your struggle to achieve your goal. You would have seen that a constant vigil on self is very necessary. Attention should be given to speech, dress, knowledge, etc. so that society gets to know our best conduct. Courage is resistance to fear and mastery of fear, not absence of fear.

> *"A great deal of talent is lost to the world for want of a little courage. Every day sends to their graves obscure man whom timidity prevented from making a first effort."*
>
> **—Sydney Smith**

❑

10

Maintaining Plus Approach—7 Strategies

"The first step towards success in any occupation is to become interested in it."

—Sir William Osler

It is a generally advocated that one should maintain a Plus Approach or Positive Attitude. However, there could be a constant struggle within oneself to do this. How can we maintain good thoughts, when our mind or body does not allow it? Often our moods do not correlate with our physical state. In fact, it is only on very few occasions that we manage to recover quickly from a depressed state.

In order to lead life effectively we have to learn to get out of our depressed state. Our mood is like a turbulent sea – sometimes we feel that we have fallen and the waves continue to crash at our heads as we fight to rise, only to be knocked down again. But the same ocean sometimes allows us to find a wave we can ride on smoothly to the shore.

The science of bio-rhythm is closely related to this subject. Primarily, in bio-rhythm, there are three cycles related to humans—the Physical, Mental and Intellectual states. These follow sinusoidal curves, and during their ascendance we feel ourselves in good spirit despite odd problems. During the descending path, the mood tends to be low and one tends to get into depression even if for very minor issues, that would otherwise have been dealt with easily. This starts from the day when we are born.

The answer to your unruly moods does not lie in meek submission, but rather in action. Action cures fears and misgivings. There are techniques which can be applied whenever our moods are erratic or we feel low.

1. Life is not always a Green Pasture

If one understands this basic philosophy, he/she can cross all hurdles. In fact, life is like a rose. The same flower that has beautiful soft petals also has sharp thorns that need careful handling. Once this fact is clear, one can face many difficulties with joy.

2. Know Your Mood

Keeping track of your moods is very essential. This will help put into perspective your ups and downs. In fact, you and only you know yourself fully. When one feels bad, it becomes difficult to imagine that things can be otherwise. Similarly, during good a period, it's amazing how quickly we forget the bad times. Hence, constant monitoring of mood is necessary.

3. Ways of Distraction

One should strive to come out of any unpleasant situation. In fact-human memory is very short, and any digression may overpower the depressive state. For this, it is important to compile a list of favorite activities which make you feel positive and optimistic. Start playing with your children, watch a movie, go for a walk or take a long breath. Often, recollecting successful or pleasant past moments helps. Laughing is also a good panacea as a distraction from any situation. Once the mood is changed, one can consequently think of solutions to the actual problems.

4. Thinking Pattern

The pattern of one's thoughts is based on the perception of an individual. It is very important to guide your mind to think the right way. It is up to you to decide whether a glass is "half full" of water or "half empty". This is how you generally see the world. So, whenever your mood is down, think positively. It will help you overcome the negative thoughts.

5. It could be Worse

Life is full of uncertainties. If you perceive that the situation could be worse than it is, the comparison could give you solace. Always try to get over your adverse moments. Recently, a gentleman was taken gravely ill, but ultimately survived. The worse scenario is that he could have died. Even though the man had a fatal disease, the fact that he survived made all the difference. Thus, any bad thought can be overpowered by comparing how the situation could have become worse. This comparison gives a lot of relief.

6. Be Hopeful

An optimistic person hopes that even the dead may stand again. His hopes are always positive. There is so much room for hope that you should program your subconscious to never give up. A popular Hindi song says "*Subah Jaroor Ayegi, Subah Ka Intjar Kar*" (Morning will definitely come, wait for it). For some persons the night may be long but the morning will definitely to arrive. It is just a matter of patience and hope.

7. Develop a Hobby

I remember someone once saying that one should have at least one addiction. Though morally this may sound quite incorrect, let's try to analyze what this person could have meant. You get addicted to something that you love and cannot do without it. In this sense, a hobby too is an addiction. So if you can indulge in a hobby, it will compulsorily help to get you into a relaxed form. Hobbies could be anything from painting, music, reading, or even controlled drinking, or meditation, or worship.

One important point is – Live with the present moment.

Now reflect on this. Can you retrieve the past? The answer is a definitely a No. What is there in the future? Can you control it? Perhaps Yes, but may be Not. So what point is there of worrying. In fact, most of us tend to spend our days either repenting for the past or thinking about the future, and in the process forget to enjoy the present moment which is so good, delightful and hopeful.

Empower your mind and soul and reap the benefits. Develop deliberateness for the same.

❑

11

Ten Steps to Upgrade Yourself

"You can't push anyone up the ladder unless he is willing to climb himself."

– Andrew Carnegie

In this competitive age, the need is to prepare yourself according to the changed environment. Job situations have become very fluid and in the private sector persons are even losing their jobs. In a scenario, maintaining the same level of competency may not yield the desired results. One has to constantly modify one's personality to keep in the so-called rat race of survival.

1. **Self-Analysis** – Are you a marketable product?
   (a) Assess whether you are capable of getting another job if you are fired.
   (b) Are your skills as per international standards? Have you developed benchmarking for yourself?
   (c) Do you update your skills to meet the changing environment?

It not realistic to assume that job security is forever. The fact is that your skills are forever. It is up to you to make yourself marketable. And to do this, follow these steps:

(a) Consider everyone for whom you are working for as a client rather than the boss.
(b) Know your potential and strengths. Exploit them to the fullest. Weaknesses should also to be identified. Then, along with a time schedule, mark out the measures to be taken for correcting these weaknesses.
(c) Always publicize your strong point in the market.
(d) The role of a specialist is not as dominant in today's world as compared to earlier times. A more generalist approach can help you reach farther. You should try to be more adaptable and flexible.

2. Fallback Skills—Develop a secondary option.

Always develop yourself to be adaptable for more than one job. In case you lose your present job and it is not possible to get the same job back, do not be caught napping. A person who is well established in a secure environment could have never imagined such a situation.

The right thing to do is to take serious cognizance of this other probability, and prepare for the same. It is necessary to develop a set of fallback skills which can enhance your portfolio. These fallback skills may never or rarely ever be used by you. But they could translate into a new career if the need arises.

3. Area of Influence—Develop Your Relational Network.

Stephan Covey has rightly emphasized upon the need for developing the area of influence. Some tricks are as under:

(a) Cultivate relationships with people other than at your workplace and nurture them.

(b) Stay in touch with them even without work. Wish them on New Year's day, birthday, etc., in order to ensure that you are concerned about them even when there is no work.

(c) Send a thank you note to the person who helps you in your hour of need.

It is common to see a person networking with people of the same profession. Try to go cross-widen your borders. Create multiple networks. This will give you a reputation of being expandable and flexible.

4. Marketing Yourself

Consider yourself as a product and constantly try project yourself to others. In other words, sell your traits. Always maintain yourself in a saleable position. For this, you have to ensure the following:

(a) People must know your capabilities and accomplishments.

(b) People must be aware of your experience.

(c) Remind others about your skills and how they can use them to their advantage. In earlier times, a person would expect to be awarded automatically if his/her job is very good. But, in this modern age, the competition is so great that it is of little use to be humble or modest about your abilities. The world is a rat race and it is very necessary for you to apprise others of your strengths or in other words, market yourself.

5. Communication Skills

Nowadays, communication skills are necessary in all walks of life. People have little spare time to listen, and your job is to communicate your point. Hence, one should develop the skill to communicate one's point to the listener in the shortest time. For this you need to think/write/talk clearly, persuasively and with impact.

6. Constant Learning

It was earlier thought that learning comes to an end once one joins a job. But nowadays this is not so. One has to be ever vigilant to the latest updates in technology, environment, economy, etc. This learning could be from one's job, from friends or acquaintances, the environment, books, magazines or Internet. It has been observed that people read very little nowadays. So, you must compulsorily allocate some time for reading, otherwise you will not be able to cope with the changes happening around you. Earlier, it was assumed that the computer was meant only for skilled computer professionals. But it is not so nowadays. The knowledge one can gain through the Internet is so immense that the computer is now more a necessity than a luxury. In fact, even a six-year-old child can operate the Internet and play computer games.

7. Develop Area of Competencies

Updating skills is the call of the day. You must have a vision of the future and upgrade yourself as per the demand. Don't just prepare for jobs but prepare for competence of the jobs. Even traditionally safe occupations are getting less and less. Everyday, fresh challenges are emerging even in so-called safe occupations like medicine and engineering.

Define yourself by what you do and how you get it done, not by your job title.

8. Treat Job as a Role

Just like a role given to an individual to perform in a drama, a job too consists of various roles like leader, problem solver, troubleshooter, counselor, mentor, etc. It is up to you how you switch from one role to the other and accord equal importance to each role. You never know which of your roles is appreciated and would give you dividend.

9. Specialist or Generalist

You can choose to be either a specialist or generalist. Both have advantages and disadvantages. If a job needs a particular knowledge, you should act as a specialist, but if more skills and knowledge are concerned, it is the job of the generalist. A generalist has a better skill portfolio and better career opportunity. But what you want to be is something that can be decided only by you after doing self-assessment. It may be noted that for both the options the set skills are different. Successful people have mentors, or they look for a mentor who takes interest in their development and don't leave them stranded for the sake of opportunity until their work is done.

10. Know Yourself

Last but not least, know yourself. Find out what you really are, what you want; where you want to go, how much time you give your family.

After applying the steps mentioned above, upgrade yourself so as to keep in the race in the competitive environment. Set realistic goals for your life and try to achieve them one by one. But remember that it may not be a smooth ride. However, remember that everything need not go smoothly, problems are bound to appear.

Congratulate yourself for the success in your efforts. Keep track of all your successes. Remember, it's these small successes that help you face larger failures and make you triumph ultimately.

❑

12

Self-Empowerment to Meet Needs of Life's Stakeholders

In modern day perspective, a person is responsible for several others like spouse, parents, brother, sister, children, friends, company, colleagues, etc. All are stakeholders for that person who has to satisfy them by his/her actions. One has to perform the role of a "joker" in the real sense and accommodate the requirements of all.

Amidst of all this, at some point of time, if you sit quietly and question yourself "Who am I" and "What do I want from my life", "What are my priorities", it will be difficult to answer these questions instantaneously. You will have to search hard to find solutions to these terse questions.

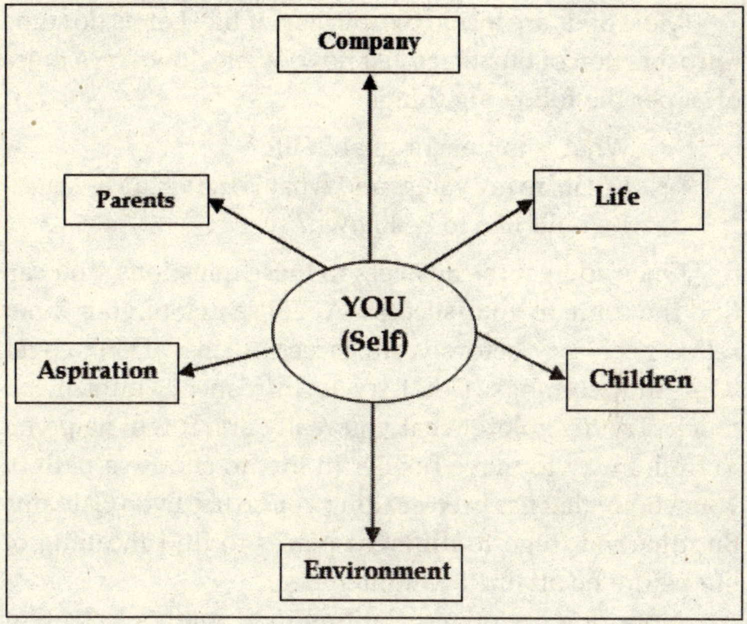

Man himself is the nerve center of all the activities in this world. He/she has to take care of self, family, company, environment, parents, children, and aspirations. The entire story moves around the self. So let us discuss about "SELF" first.

It has been found that we try to find the answer of these nagging questions many times during the course of our life.

- In what direction should I go?
- How do I focus and get clarity in life?
- What is the goal of my life?

If one can answer these questions, he/she can formulate a strategy for life and the goal of life.

Rudyard Kipling once wrote:

> *"People say that what we are all seeking is the meaning of life. I think that what we are really seeking is the experience of being alive."*

Most of us are lost in the journey of life. Let us do some retrospection of ourselves just now. Write down on a piece of paper the following things:

- What is my major goal in life?
- What are my values and what is the virtue by which I would like to be known?

Once you get the answers to these questions, you can find the route to your success. A real search of your inner self is necessary before you proceed further. Don't cover your shortcomings. Don't try to introspect yourself too much. Try to explore what you really are. It will help you to find a way to move further in life, to choose a path of your choice that has been evading you so far. Even Gautama Buddha had to go to different places to find meaning of life before he attained enlightenment.

Note down your revelations in a notebook, so that whenever you see it, you are reminded of the commitments you have made to yourself. No commitment is higher than the commitment you make to yourself. In fact, if the theory is used properly with our children, then we can find the areas where they excel, and their energy can be channelized to achieve the goal.

> *"You cannot teach a man anything; You can only help him to find it within himself."*
>
> **–Galileo**

Explore yourself in a calm and quiet place, may be you can meet your real self.

Co-ordination

Here is an old story, which has its value in real life, that is, if one can take advantage of it.

"There was a poor student, who was supposed to participate in a program, and was asked to wear short pants as the costume. The boy did not possess short pants. His mother and sister told him not to worry about it, though they were very concerned. As they did not want the boy to know what they were up to, they waited for him to go to sleep. Then, during the night the mother woke up and cut up the boy's full pants to nearly half and went back to sleep. After some time the sister got up and cut up the pants to half the size."

The readers can derive result. Thus, proper co-ordination is very essential in life, so that many small or big mishaps are averted. Whether it is the office or home or anywhere else, one should try to have proper co-ordination in what is being done, taking into view all the parameters.

Thief Theory

When a thief goes to steal, he intends to be a winner, i.e. to have a good theft. Wherever he attempts he tries to be successful. The purpose in the normal sense may be negative, but for him it is a goal to achieve.

The classical part of the theft is that the thief can loot any house, whatsoever may be the security system. How it is done and what sort of technique is to be employed for that particular theft, is best known only to the thief. The analogy is that—the thief attacks at the weakest point of the target place.

Similarly to tackle any situation, try to employ the "Thief Theory". Try to find the weakest point of the situation and attack at that point and win over the situation.

"While goals are chosen, a purpose is discovered.
Our purpose is something we have been doing

all along and will continue to do, regardless of circumstances, until we die."

—Peter Mechwilliams

Self versus Shareholders

As explained above, an individual is responsible for a diverse group. Meeting the aspirations of such a diverse group can be difficult as the demand of each individual could be different.

One school of thought is that you should concentrate only on your own self-interest and have only a secondary look at the other stakeholders which includes family and parents. You might have come across such persons, but would you rate them as successful or otherwise? These groups have tremendous power over self. However, they tend to satisfy those stakeholders who would otherwise go against them. But concentrating on satisfying the needs of specific stakeholders may also be detrimental in the overall success level.

Excelling in one area is not a certificate of success. One has to strike a balance between self and other stakeholders. Thus, a middle path should be followed, i.e. 70 per cent concentration on self-development and 30 per cent on others. A proper strategy for this will have to be drawn by the individual for this.

One should manage oneself the same way as one would manage a firm. Imaging yourself as a product in the market and that you have to sell yourself in this competitive environment. Make yourself saleable. You are your own CEO. It is up to you how you manage yourself.

Positive Economic Value of Self

In order to manage life, we can employ present management techniques and one of them is Value-based

Management. Let us see how this can be implemented in our life.

This technique lays emphasis on improving upon the Economic Value of Self (EVS). It is the annual valuation of yourself after all expenditures in financial terms and qualities you develop within yourself. It is based on following parameters:

1. Measurements

We have to develop tools of measurement for our financial and quality capabilities. This can be done on annual basis. The endeavor should be to have enhancement at earlier levels. It would be better to assess the income. Accordingly, budget allocation to all the expenditures could be done. Further, a provision for saving should be envisaged on annual basis to the order of 33 per cent of the income. Regular measurements are necessary.

2. Corrective action can be taken.

3. Motivation

This life is yours; no one else can take care of it. Only you know your strengths and weaknesses. Thus, own yourself and your stakeholders perfectly, as no one else will take care of your family, your aspirations, etc. The concept is that, by taking care of your stakeholders, you get motivated by that success. A perfect successful person is one who satisfies the needs of the environment as well as of oneself.

4. Management System

You have to devise your own system of managing your life. You may have to develop a priority system for handling issues. Let's take an example. Suppose your wife needs attention, just then there is a call from your mother. How would you handle the situation so that both are satisfied? You definitely need to have some strategy to handle such situations and also understand the consequences thereof.

5 Mindset

This is one of the important parameters in everyone's life. It is ideal if a common mindset is developed among family members. Different mindset leads to conflicts. Rigidity and adamancy have to be avoided. A positive mindset is the best quality of an individual. Always try to do the right thing at the right place and right time for better utilization of energy and time.

Try to evaluate yourself based on the above parameters and develop Positive Economic Value of Self. It is an index of success.

Competitive Advantage

From the above it is clear that it is very important to have continuous edge over the competitors. Here, the competitors are not only in your profession, but interestingly also at the family front—your brothers, sisters and other relatives. In day-to-day life, often a financially sound relative carries more weight than others. He tends to have more value than others in the eyes of many. But this does not mean there is no hope for the person who is less financially off. The crux is to acquire other virtues and prove you are better than others. Follow the following steps to acquire competitive advantage.

(a) **Be Different.** Always tries to be different than others. At work, it is often observed that the boss appreciates those individuals who are able to supplement him in his work. Try to find out which are the areas where the boss needs your help. Sharpen that skill and update yourself accordingly. In case skill in computers is required, and you don't have it, then go and acquire computer knowledge. Else your competitor will leave you behind in the race.

(b) **Credibility or reliability** is similarly the virtue which differentiates you from others. Why not be more reliable or credible?

The above aspects can be developed in the following way:

(i) **Knowledge of Self**: Knowing yourself is the most important aspect of life. You should be able to decipher your strengths and your weaknesses. Remember, this again depends upon the circumstances. For example, your strength may be that of going into details about a situation. But if your find that you have to be precise during a particular situation and detailing needs to be avoided, then the strength becomes a weakness.

(ii) **Understand the Requirement:** Knowledge and understanding of a situation is very essential to regulate behavior. Many people grumble that they have done right things but their bosses did not appreciate them. Why it is so? Why is it that the target we shoot is not what our bosses want? This lacuna is not limited to just the office but sometimes happens in our family also. To avoid this shortcoming, study the requirements of the situation and understand how best you should act on it.

(iii) **Armor Yourself** Consider this life is a war. Based on the requirements of the situation, armor yourself with different gadgets and use them judiciously. Only then will you be able to sustain the battle of life. You have to change the strategy of war each time. But remember that unlike the Bhagavad Gita, there is no Krishna to guide or help out. Even if you get help from others occasionally, you and only you have to fight your war. So, a strategy is to be devised how it can be done and how the battle can be won. Whether it is a technical, social or financial challenge, update yourself as the situation demands.

(iv) **Quick Response** In this modern age, quick resolution of problems and fast reaction to them is the order of the day. Quick response refers to the speed with which you react to a situation and take a decision. This can be done only if you are conscious of the circumstances and surroundings and adapt accordingly. The speed with which you respond to an unexpected challenge is the key to success. It will give you competitive advantage, and of course your performance will also improve.

(v) **Synergy with Others** Man is a social being and a lone man cannot lead an isolated life. So, do not hesitate to take help from any quarter. You have to develop synergy with others in different areas of activities. It is often seen that people tend to be adamant against seeking help as they feel they do not want to bow down to anyone. Forget your ego. In the present perspective, everybody needs someone or the other. You never know when you may need the help of a person you would normally shun. So, identify persons whom you can trust. Make a team for the work and then strike the target. Success cannot evade you.

If you introspect, you'll find that the value of self is so powerful that you can acquire all the required virtues by the time you achieve your goal successfully. But you need develop some inherent qualities within yourself for a successful life.

The question here is – who is successful, a wealthy man, a happy man or someone else? Is it possible to define who is a successful person? Putting it simply, success is nothing but ABC – Ability, Beliefs and Courage. Intrinsically, success is the courage to start and willingness to keep it everlasting. To succeed one must possess an effective combination of ability, ambition, courage, drive, hard work, integrity and loyalty. Is it easy to have so many virtues within one man? Yes, definitely so. Most successful persons possess most, if not all, the mentioned qualities. If we can reach up to these bench markers, we are on our way to becoming successful. Merely being wealthy, professionally sound or having other possessions does not make a person successful in the true sense. Winston Churchill has said, "Success is never final, you have to keep earning it over and over again."

A successful person is one who acquires all-round progress and is able to satisfy his stakeholders like family members, friends, society, etc.

Let us discuss some of the virtues required for being successful.

Leadership

Look at the leadership qualities of history's greats like Mahatma Gandhi, Lal Bahadur Shastri, Jay Prakash Narayan, Jack Welch of GE, or Bill Gates of Microsoft. They are leaders whom people follow without asking any questions. Their stories are known to most of us. Such leaders are few in numbers, but without them something would be definitely amiss. Till his death Mahatma Gandhi did not leave his mission. India's another pre-Independence leader Lok Manya Tilak was editing a newspaper when he got the message of the death of his son. Tilak kept the message aside, completed his editing work, and then went home to share his grief with his family.

The qualities of these leaders are something different from what others possess. Nothing stops us from trying to match them. If you have them as role modes, you can also aspire to succeed as a leader.

Herb Khelleher of America's Southwestern Airlines said,

> "I describe leadership as servanthood. The best leader, I think, has to be a good follower as well. You have to be quite willing to accept other people's ideas, even though they are in conflict with your own. If you won't fight for your people, then you can't count on your people not fighting for you."

Leadership needs some virtues so that the followers can appreciate them. It is worth mentioning here that there are many followers, but proper leadership is in short supply.

Leaders are successful because they do the right things at the right time— both personally and within the organization and within society. Some of the virtues required for developing as a good leader are as follows:

1. Self-sacrifice

In Indian conditions, leaders are worshipped like God. They see in them idealism, honesty, integrity and self-sacrificing nature. An example is cited below.

Herb Kelleher of the South West Airline used to sit at the ticket counter, even as his employees enjoyed festival leave. It is nothing but self-sacrifice by this great American businessman who did not mind doing any job that would lead him to his goal. In fact, leadership thrives only when one forgets his/her own interests. How many persons are there who can do that? That's the reason why there is a shortage of leaders nowadays.

In India too people worship their leaders and follow them blindly, but it does not take them too long to do a volte face if they find their leader to be tainted. In January 1989, the public lauded the honesty and integrity of V.P. Singh who was sworn as the new prime minister. A few months later, in November that year, the same public criticized immensely for his policies on the controversial Mandal Commission Report.

Here is an example of a former ICS officer Aurobindo Ghosh. After resigning from service, Ghosh was burdened with mounting expenditure due to studies of his two brothers. He met the monetary requirements, but did not shy from even sleeping on roadsides and doing hard labor. Such self-sacrifice is sometimes necessary.

The idea is to develop the tendency for self-sacrifice for the cause of others.

2. Passion for the Purpose

This is one of the most desired features a leader must have. It is a virtue which can be developed gradually. Most modern leaders of industry in the United States have a passion they share with their people and their companies.

Elizabeth Dole of American Red Cross said, "Having a passion for what you do, a sense of mission that comes from the heart, gives you energy, drive and enthusiasm that contagious and essential for leading an organization."

Bill Gates of Microsoft supports Dole and said, *"I have the most of fun job in this world, and love coming to work each day. There are always new challenges, new opportunities and new things to learn. If you enjoy your job this much, you never burn out."*

Bob Eaton of Daimler Chrysler said, "I tell young adults, 'You have to be excited about going to work and trying to have an impact'."

David Johnson of Campbell Soup said, "Go out and do whatever you want to do. Don't wait and don't look for approval. And don't sit around what will happen next. Push the pedal to the metal and most of life. Life is not a dress rehearsal. This is our life. This is dying—Tick, Tick, Tick. What are you doing to make most of it?"

So it is clear that all great successful leaders had passion for their purpose. Take the case of Mahatma Gandhi. Despite all the atrocities by the English government, he did not deviate from his purpose and finally gained freedom for India. Nelson Mandela of South Africa fought against apartheid and ultimately succeeded in his purpose after being imprisoned for 20 odd years.

What all this shows is that dreaming for leadership is good, but to be a real leader requires some qualities which need to be consciously developed within ourselves.

3. Integrity and Honesty

Both these words are most talked about, but how far one can achieve them depends upon the individual. In the present context, absoluteness in both the parameters may not be possible but it can be achieved by and large.

A small boy in Baghdad used to go on the streets to sell some items. One day he found that he could not sell enough to buy him even his dinner for that night. Under distress he started offering his ware at cheaper rate. After a lot of effort, the boy managed to sell his goods. But the buyer had only a note of big denomination and not enough coins to pay. The boy requested the man to take the item, and promised the buyer that he would return the balance money at his home. The next day the buyer did not receive the balance money, and went looking for the boy. He managed to locate the younger brother of the boy who explained that his brother had met with an accident while he was on his way to the gentleman's home to return the money. The boy was admitted in hospital in a critical state. The overwhelmed man went to the hospital, and impressed by the integrity and honesty of the young boy, adopted him.

The moral is: Honesty and integrity is appreciated by all and can also change the minds.

By and large, an honest person is liked by everybody and most leaders in India like Mahatma Gandhi, Sardar Patel, and Lal Bahadur Shastri were liked by the people for their integrity and honesty.

Living with integrity and leading by example is the internal sense of right and wrong, and this is what should direct a person. Everybody should have 100 per cent control over it, and certainly a successful person does. Integrity builds trust in the environment. It is rightly said that integrity is the first ingredient for success. You may have integrity and still fail, but the opposite is not true. This formula is prevalent worldwide. In a study conducted in the United States, it was observed that all business leaders pointed out those employees who spent a lot of time watching what their boss does. Here the boss becomes the example or leader for their subordinates.

- Integrity for self
- Honesty for purpose and people.

It is a misnomer that honesty pertains to money only. It also relates to other areas. Honesty for the purpose is the most desired quality of leaders. This includes honesty for the people working for him, like giving credit to those who deserve.

Fisher, CEO of The Gap, USA says, "*Credit should go where it belongs*". What an honest confession.

Herb Kelleher of Southwest Airline takes this concept of a leader, "The best leaders have to be good followers as well". He says, "You have to be willing to accept other people idea, even when they are in conflict with your own. You have to be willing to subjugate your ego to the needs of your business. You have to be selfless and take risks for your people. If you won't fight for the people, then you can count on your people not fighting with you."

"A leader is someone who can take a group of people to a place they don't think they go."

—Bob Eaton,
Chairman of Daimler Chrysler, USA

4. Vision

Earlier it was advocated that one should not be a daydreamer but night dreaming was allowed. But the fact is that it is good to dream big as this can make you achieve the height you want. One should not be a miser in dreaming. Dreams do not cost anything, but requires a vision.

All prominent leaders have long vision or big ideas with a winning strategy. In this competitive environment where we daily witness many companies shutting down, many getting acquired and many more getting merged, a leader must have a winning strategy. In order to survive in the market, Jack Welch of GE shifted from Products to Services, where he found more margins. The same analogy also goes to individuals. One should frequently change the strategy for survival in this competitive world.

Not only must leaders come up with a big idea, it must be the right big idea. The leaders need to go to the roots and build on the things that are required for self, organization or country. The leaders have to have long sightedness, only then can they devise the strategy. They have to be visionaries.

5. Working as a Team

This concept is told to everyone on the job, but the results are not commensurate with the concept. Take the case of the Indian cricket team. Each individual is excellent, but when it comes to team spirit, we often see they are not able to succeed. Michael Dell of Dell Computers says, "One person cannot do anything alone." Steve Case of American Online says, "There is one-to-one correlation with the quality of the people on a particular project and quality of the project's leader. Since companies are really a collection of people, results can be tied directly to the quality of the management team."

In a team, the strengths are exploited and the weaknesses covered by mutual strengths. Thus, a team having more strength will win in any case. All team members have to contribute to their best, and the victory or loss is that of the team and not of any individual. Everybody shares the fruit.

Even the world leadership nowadays impresses upon team-concept. The team may have two or more members. On the home front too, if the husband and wife make a team and proceed to work together, that house will flourish, contrary to a house where the couple has different priorities.

A team therefore has a single priority. Sharing the same priority, the team members focus on the target with their fullest energy and the outcome is generally victory. They work together for achieving the common goal of the team and not of any individual. The team leader has to inculcate the feeling of team spirit, and see that individual team members keep their own interests as a last priority. The principal of building great management teams involve continuous evolution and pruning, if necessary.

6. Inspiring Others

Any leader is successful only when the follower understands his/her vision, theory and style. The leader has to be down to earth and without any ego. Don Fisher of The GAP USA says, "Check your ego at the door. Don't arrive and think that you are everything".

A good leader should take the people along in the job, not ask the people to get along. If you are not able to take the people along with you, then your leadership quality is at question.

If the leader has to be successful, he has to attack on the sensitive emotions of human beings. A successful leader takes charge of these sensitive points and learns to understand and know his/her followers. The first premise of successful leadership is to consider that by and large everyone is okay. If you take care of the people they will also see that your interests are protected. You have to only keep a close eye on them. Create an environment where people enjoy working. An employee should come to office with a smiling face, with the idea in mind that he/she has to contribute something for the growth of the company. This will make them more productive. This is possible only if the people are constantly inspired for the work.

When subordinates are made to understand about their importance and value for the job at hand, they are bound to deliver the goods. It is up to the leaders to see how to influence them. It is often heard that "people have different levels of desires, but directionally, they want the same kind of things. They want to be respected and have a sense of being dealt with fairly. At every level, they want to make a contribution and be recognized for it." This sounds like a nominal requirement, but how many of us do it for our employees.

This adage holds true for our house too. If the husband appreciates his wife for cooking up a good recipe, she would surely be encouraged to offer even better food. So the idea is to dole out compliments for a job well done. This should not be a one-time effort, but a continuous process and requires a lot of perseverance. Good leaders are generally determined to make the follower understand them and don't leave till the objectives are met. So, communicate continuously, listen carefully, genuinely tolerate failure as a learning experience, build on people's desires, and make a positive difference. The challenge of a leader is to unleash the energy of the people and harness it towards the goal.

> *"A leader, once convinced that a particular course of action is the right one, must...be undaunted when the going gets though."*
>
> **—Ronald Reagan**

❑

13

Stress Management Techniques

"Read books, listen to tapes, attend seminar – they are decades of wisdom reduced to invaluable hours.

– Mark Victor Hansen

What is Stress?

People have their own definitions for this term, as it does not have a single meaning. It is individual based. Different people get stressed at different conditions. It depends upon their Stress Tolerance Limit (STL). The need is to enhance the limit of STL. Stress has direct impact on the health of a person. In this competitive world, nobody can escape from stress. Perhaps, even ascetics (*sadhus*), other than those who meditate in the wilderness, get stressed due to their surrounding and the increasing number of disciples who throng them.

In a common man's life, stress areas are as under:

(1) Profession
(2) Finance and Property
(3) Life Partner
(4) Children
(5) Parents

These are the major areas from where stress starts. Let us take the example of a professional having an engineering degree and a good job, and describe the stress points he could face.

1. Professional Stress

It is very difficult to achieve success in your working life if your profession is not as per your choice. Let's take a situation when you do not get any promotion despite putting in hard work, and your juniors surpass you. This surely leads to stress. Suppose you get an untimely transfer to a place which is not of your choice—stress again. You are assigned jobs that are not are of your choice—yet another stressful situation. If your frequency does not match with that of your boss and he reprimands you throughout out the day, it surely is stressful for you. There may be many more instances in professional life that put you in stress.

2. Finance and Property

This is one of the main causes of stress. If you don't own your own house or you have growing-up children, you get stressed because you are not able to cope with the increasing financial needs of the family. If your bank balance is not enough to finance children's education and you want to admit your child in the best school of the city, you can get stressed. It may be noted that the stress generated in this area also affects other areas of life. It has been observed that if a person is financially well-off, the stress from other areas gets covered up and is not so painful. This is because the person feels relieved that he/she is at least financially secure.

3. **Life Partner**

After attaining adulthood and getting a job, one usually gets married. Nowadays, married life has become very fragile due to intolerance of individuals. The wife wants to go for a job and her husband thinks otherwise. This is a stressful condition for both. In another scenario, the wife feels her husband is not paying attention to her and spends more time in his profession—again there is stress.

4. Children

They are cause for stress most often. This can be illustrated as under for better comprehension:

- You don't get a child after marriage—*Stress.*
- You get a child but it is deformed—*Stress.*
- You get a girl child whereas you wanted a boy—*Stress.*
- You get two consecutive daughters instead of a son—*Stress.*
- You have a son as you wished, but he is not good in studies—*Stress.*
- You want your child to be an all-rounder, but he/she is good only in studies, not in other activities—*Stress.*
- Your child is good in studies, but cannot get admission in a professional school of your choice—*Stress.*
- Your child is professionally qualified, but is not getting married—*Stress.*

- Gets married but relationship with partner is not good—*Stress.*
- Married but not taking care of parents—*Stress.*

Thus, there is stress at every point.

5. Parents

Last but not least, parents are the cause for stress in most of the middle-class families in India. After marriage when you are not able to take care of your parents due to professional engagements or any other reason, it breeds stress. When you are not able to attend to them when they are sick, it causes stress. When they need you to resolve a problem and you are not able to be present, it causes a stressful condition as you are emotionally attached to them and circumstances are not favorable for you to attend to them.

From the above it is clear that the cause of stress in most of the cases is:

1. You want it, or in other words you want a thing to happen, or
2. You want the event to be as per your desire.

Are you stressed? This is the first and foremost question which could be answered only by you. Here are some actions that act as stress indicators.

- Do you get angry spontaneously?
- Do you blame others for any problem?
- Do you have fear of others?
- Do you feel anxiety throughout the day?
- Do you generally feel tensed?
- Do you generally feel depressed?
- Do you generally feel fatigue?

If the answer is YES for more than 50 per cent of the above questions, then you live under stress due to one thing or another, and there is need to identify the stress areas.

Identifying Stress Points

This is one of the main exercises to be done before introduction of any improvement technique. Truthful answers would help you in your development. So, be truthful to yourself.

List out the stress points in all categories mentioned below:

(a) Profession
(b) Finance and Property
(c) Life Partner
(d) Children
(e) Parents

Corrective action can be taken only after identification.

Stress is also a Motivator.

This is not surprising. An anecdote is being narrated here to supplement this view. Some 10 years ago I had been invited to read the palm of a gentleman. As I studied his palm I saw some lines crossing each other while some were not very clear. This indicated that he was undergoing some tension. When I told him this, he promptly replied that tension is good for him, and that if he did not have tension, he would not be able to move ahead, and there would be no progress. He said tension was his driving force. I was awakened by the answer. I now realize that stress can be converted into a motivator, provided the individual wants it so. The idea is to convert negative stress to positive stress.

Suppose you have to complete some work by a specified date, then you may worry whether you will be able to complete the work by that date, or whether you will get support from others, etc. Such signals give rise to negative stress.

Let us consider the same situation when there is positive approach to the job. You take it as a challenge to complete the work by the target. The resources have to be arranged only by you. You will try to get help from different quarters after identifying the resources. Your aim is to complete the work. Thus, the date which alarmed another person, acts as a motivator to you to complete the work for your internal satisfaction. The fact is that under positive stress conditions the performance of a person is more enhanced than normal.

Similarly, other situations can also be converted into positive stress. Then the problem will become a project and you will be able to win over the situation. So, try to convert negative stress into positive stress.

Stress Management Techniques

India has used stress management techniques from times immemorial. Example can be drawn from the epic Bhagavad Gita where Arjuna is stressed in the battlefield because he has to kill his kith and kin, including his teachers in the battlefield. Arjuna is not able to bear the thought and succumbs to stress. At this point Lord Krishna counsels Arjuna through different techniques and ultimately gets Arjuna to agree to fight. To take another example, the Indian cricket team has succumbed to stress for a consecutive nine times in the finals of different tournaments. The players were not able to cope with the pressures and their performance was affected. But they pulled themselves together again and again through motivation.

Stress attacks mainly the mind, both conscious and subconscious. Brain is the nerve center of all action and if it is attacked by the stress virus then the formatting of the brain gets disturbed and our actions are distorted accordingly. Hence, you need to keep the brain and mind in its optimum level of functioning. So the techniques of stress management should focus more on keeping the brain fit.

"Thealm" is one of the ideal techniques for stress management. Let's see what it is:

1. **T**ime Management.
2. **H**obby Development.
3. **E**ating Habits.
4. **A**erobic-Breathing Exercises.
5. **L**et-it-Be Concept.
6. **M**editative techniques.

1. Time Management

Time is one of the main factors which trouble the people of metropolitan cities, where most people are under stress. People are always rushing around and time once gone never comes back. Due to lack of proper time management, most people find it difficult to finish work on time. This causes stress to the individuals. In this competitive age, everyone seems to be in a blind race. When you open your eyes, you will find a throng of people both ahead and behind. If you try to retrace your steps, you will be trampled by the people behind. The only solution is move further. If you decide to slow down you may not be able to reach the target on time, and if you try to move faster, your strength will ebb. Thus, time causes stress. Interestingly, as you move farther, you will keep meeting a different groups of people from different categories to deal with. This goes on till one day you hit a dead wall and cannot move further. You become stagnant and this causes more stress as others move ahead of you.

So, the need is to manage time according to your requirement. Some methods of time management are given below:

a) **A-B-C Analysis of Work**: The works can be divided as per the time priority and time requirement. Divide the work into:

A–Type: Most important–to be given first priority.

B–Type: Lesser important–to be prioritized as second.

C–Type: Least important–to be done last.

Most successful people know the art of prioritization of work. It is not necessary to do all the work by yourself. You should also know:

- The work which is to be dumped.
- The work which is to be delegated.
- The work which is to be done by you.

You should do only those works by yourself that which require your inputs or attention. Otherwise delegate the work.

In order to manage time, first of all maintain a diary of the work and allocate it as required.

Do forward planning so that time is not wasted at the last moment. You could have target dates of different activities and try to carry out the same before time. This will control the anxiety which might happen due to non-completion of the work on time, and stress is avoided.

Stop being Perfectionist

Achieving perfection is a malice of executives. Perfection is good but obsession for it leads to stressful conditions. Those who are after this are mostly stressed, because due to their attitude, they want perfection everywhere–it may be at work, home or anywhere. Everybody cannot become No. 1 in the company, everybody cannot become famous. So it is best to expand up to the boundary where you are under emotional control and without stress. For example everybody wants to good education to their children and there are schools with different range of fees. If your salary is ₹ 10000 per month and the fees are ₹ 3000, how you can afford the expenditure? It would be better to get the child admitted in a school with fees in the affordable range. Thus, if you can compromise just one level below than the perfection, most of us will be stress-free.

Time for Family

You feel your family has done a lot for your development. So, if sufficient time is not given to them you may get stressed. Introspect yourself and find out how much time you give your family every day, and how much time you share with your life partner. In fact, most successful people try to have at least dinner with their family and in the worst scenario, all the family members meet during lunch time on Sundays. In Indian conditions where family ties are very strong, it is necessary to devote sufficient time for the family. How you manage it, is up to you.

Time for Yourself

You need to cull out some time for yourself. You keep yourself busy through the day/month/year either for your job or for others. Do you have any time for yourself? In a day, take out some time for yourself wherein you can reflect about your physical and mental development. It may be just for 15 minutes, but try to cull it out for yourself. Iterative exercises need to be done for analyzing self, and continuous corrective action needs to be taken.

2. Hobbies

The other effective measures for stress management are hobbies like yoga, reading, listening music, painting, etc. In fact, you should develop some hobbies which you can pursue in your leisure time. Listening to music of your choice is a stress reliever. When under stress, see a movie of your choice—the stressed phase will fade away. If you are under stress for many days, it is good to go on a tour to a hill station or any tourist place. It will break the monotony and there will be relief from the stressed conditions. Doing yoga in the morning is again a good tool for relieving stress.

3. Eating Habits

In the ancient Indian texts, a person is said to have three *Gunas*: (a) *Rajo Guna,* (b) *Sato Guna,* and (c) *Tamo Guna.* Stress is co-related to *Tamo Guna*. A person having *Tamo Guna* is more susceptible to stress. Food which develops *Tamo Guna* tendencies are meat, spices, alcohol and drugs. So, in order to have less stress, the eating habits have to change. During the stress period, it is better to be vegetarian as the food is easily digestible and less toxic, but at the same time contain most nutritional value. If you maintain your digestive system in a proper condition, ailments shall keep away from you. In a human body, there are only two points from where ailments start: (a) stomach and (b) mind.

The condition of the mind depends on the stomach, so first of all the digestive system has to function properly. Often, overwork and anxiety leads to acidity, constipation, etc. This has direct effect on the mind and you become stressed. By changing eating habits to suit the body, you can strive to have a healthy body, and thus a healthy mind. It is therefore advised to have fibrous food with plenty of green vegetables.

Blood thickening also plays an important role in stress-related illnesses. Patients with blood pressure are given blood-thinning medicines such as aspirin. These medicines facilitate the thinning of the blood so that the flow through the artilleries becomes smooth and the heart functions properly. Stress causes blood pressure which forms a cycle of cause and effect, so it is good to reduce the blood thickness and maintain ideal blood pressure. Avoid taking foodstuff having Vitamin K, like tomatoes, etc.

So eating habits can be changed to prevent the stressful conditions. Be a vegetarian by and large.

4. **Aerobic-Breathing Exercises**

This is one of the best techniques for releasing stress. There is nothing new in this concept, but it needs to be understood. In breathing, we inhale oxygen which oxygenates the blood, thus purity of the blood increases. This results in more energy for our body.

Lungs and heart are two vital organs of the body. The blood gets oxygenated and purified in the lungs. The pulmonary vein brings the purified, oxygen-rich blood from the lungs to the left auricle of the heart.

Lungs have bronchioles and each bronchiole ends in a small sac called air sac. These sacs contain microscopic cavities called Alveoli. The alveoli have extremely thin walls, covered by blood capillaries. When the inhaled air reaches the alveoli, oxygen is absorbed by it. Oxygen then passes from the wall of the alveoli into the blood vessel, the blood gets oxygenated and the cycle continues likewise.

It is most important to understand that the more fresh air we take in, the more oxygen gets into the blood. This in turn breaks the glucose of the blood into energy, and carbon dioxide released as an end-product is carried by the blood vessel back to the alveoli from where it is expelled through the nostrils.

Long breathing exercises lead to more intake of oxygen, more energy and less stress and we become more energetic and develop the power to fight against stress.

Whenever you undergo stress, do the following exercises:

(i) Inhale and count 1 to 6.
(ii) Hold the breath, count 1-2-3.
(iii) Exhale, counting 1 to 12 slowly.

This means the exhale time should be twice that of inhale time, depending on the capacity of the lungs. By practicing this exercise 21 times, particularly in the morning when fresh air is available, it can yield excellent results. After doing this for 21 days, you will find a complete change in your attitude. Some changes include development of positive attitude, better decision making, less stress and better handling of situations. Just develop belief in the system. It is panacea for all your problems in life.

5. Let-It-Be Concept

This is one of the best tools for reducing the stress condition of the mind. One thing is as sure in life—stress is bound to happen. No person on earth is free from it at some point of life. For some it may be less, and for others it may be more.

Taking things seriously may cause more stress whereas considering the situation "Let it be" may reduce the degree of tension. Every problem gets solved one day or the other, patience is necessary. So, have patience and reduce the stress level.

6. Meditation

This term is known to most, but the need is to understand the concept. The origin of the word can be traced from the Latin word "Meditari" which has as its root "Mederi" meaning to heal. So, meditation can be said to be the science of healing all physical and mental ailments. If you meditate just on the advise of some Guru or spiritual teacher, it may not have as much impact as it would if you understand the impact of what you are going. Doing something after knowing the theory behind it can garner better results.

Briefly the theory of meditation is as under:

When our mind concentrates on something for a considerable period time, meditation occurs. By this, we try to control our thought process which normally wavers. There is an increase in productivity if work is done with concentration. To start with, deliberate attempt is needed to concentrate, but later it becomes easier. According to Patanjali, *Dhyana* is focusing the mind on some chosen object or subject, and meditation involves a long stretch of *Dhyana*.

By meditating, stress gets released and the mind freshens up. It also has an impact on the subconscious mind, where all the information is stored and registered. Meditation is the technique to format the subconscious mind. This helps to keep all the information in a proper form in the mind and avoids the interference of one with another.

In higher techniques of meditation, concentration is done on the six *chakras* located in the body. These *chakras* are located at different places in the brain and spinal cord and are not visible to eye. They are said to affect the glands which secrete different hormones into the blood, and different psychic powers are attributed to them. Each hormone performs a specific function inside the body and by meditation, discharge of different juices is regulated. When juices are discharged in a proper manner, the physical, mental and emotional growth of the person will also get regulated. Further, when the *chakras* get charged, sublimate energy is released.

Before going ahead, it is essential to understand the co-relation of glands and *charkas*.

S.No.	Gland	Location	Type of Hormone Secreted	Corresponding *Chakras*
1.	Pineal	Behind the brain	Called Third Eye develops hormone Melatonin that is responsible for day/night cycle, aging etc.	*Sahasrara*
2.	Pituitary	Behind the brain	Master gland that controls activity of all other glands	*Ajan*
3.	Thyroid	In the neck	Secretes hormone Thyroxin which helps in body growth	*Visuddha*
4.	Thymus	Near the heart under breast bone	Secretes hormone for development of immune system	*Anahata*
5.	Pancreas	Near navel	Secretes hormone insulin which controls blood sugar	*Manipura*
6.	Adrenal	Above kidneys	Secretes hormone Adrenaline when a person is under stress	*Swathisthan*
7.	Prostrate	Near the joint of legs	Responsible for developing sex energy	*Muladhara*

We can understand that the glands have specific relation with the *Chakras* and by meditation the secretion of juices from the glands gets regulated. The total body gets revitalized and energized while meditating, and this keeps us hale and hearty, the Stress Tolerance Limit get enhanced and even the effect of age on the face/body can reduce. The basic technique for meditation is to simply concentrate on the glands in sequence starting from the lowest up. This can be done for at least three minutes each. After this let the thoughts come and go; you will find a change in your total system.

Meditation can be done at any time, preferably where there are fewer disturbances. However, when you actually sit to meditate you will find that there are more disturbances inside your mind than outside. You can sit in any comfortable. Meditation can also be done with light music as it attenuates the surrounding noises. Chants of AUM, light sitar music, etc. can be used. It would be good to wear loose clothes. Meditation is best medication for stress.

To conclude, stress management is a very important aspect of life and every individual should endeavor to develop their own methodology to do it as per requirement.

❑

14

Self-Boundary Management

Nowadays, a new word discussed frequently in management circles is "Boundary Management". Its meaning is quite clear that one should manage his/her boundaries. Weak boundaries may face ingression by outsiders. In a wider perspective, India as a country has to manage the boundaries with neighborhood countries like Pakistan, Bangladesh and Nepal. On the industrial front, take the case of a mega company like Reliance. Its progress story tells about their excellence in boundary management. Similarly, personal success also depends largely on managing the outside world like superiors at work, associates, relations, etc.

Let us discuss the concept of Self-Boundary Management for an individual. Individually, a person is a unique being. No one can match another, but a few do become iota of success in life. Their examples are being taken everywhere, as they become references of success in different fields. Apart from labor, determination and luck, their boundary management is also excellent. Let's determine the factors responsible for boundary management for a professional person.

(1) Professional Area:

(a) Boss
(b) Super boss
(c) Other environment

(2) Home front:

(a) Life partner
(b) Parents, in-laws and other relations

(3) Living Environment: Neighbors

(4) Friends and Associates

"Good timber does not grow with ease; the stronger the wind, the stronger the tree."

—J. Willard Marriott

1. Boss

For a professional, the boss is nothing less than God, whose pen is said to be mightier than the sword. So the fact is that when you get a job and start working, you have to learn to manage with your boss. It is a matter of making a rapport.

The ability to establish rapport is one of the most important skills a person can have. In fact, rapport makes any task simpler, easier and more enjoyable. Rapport is nothing but entering and understanding someone else's world. You must understand the requirements of the boss and style of functioning. Most often, people tend to work according to their own convenience. This has to be corrected.

In fact, the correct word is "tuning" which means matching of frequencies. You might have observed that when you switch on the radio, a particular station is tuned only when the transmitting and receiving frequencies are the same. Similarly, by understanding the frequency of your boss, you can develop a rapport with the boss.

2. **Super Boss**

The role of super boss is equally important. He is a person who may not be in direct touch with you, but has information about you. This information needs to be correct; otherwise although you are in-tune with your boss, you can get phased out with the super boss. In case the boss and super boss are out of tune with each other, then the situation can get grimmer. You have to manage your boundaries as per the situation. In these circumstances, a successful person may come out with laurels without hurting anybody. It is worth mentioning here that the techniques employed are totally individualistic and depends on circumstances. It is really an art. You should try to market yourself as a product and advertise the features of the product to the boss or super boss or to anyone else only after employing suitable marketing techniques.

3. Others

This area basically covers others who are not directly connected with your job, but who have a say in the organization. They may not be able to benefit you directly but their one word can harm you. It should be your endeavor to see that nobody in the organization speaks negatively against you. The key word in this regard is to "understand" them. Abraham Lincoln rightly said, "If you would win a man to your cause, first convince him you are his real friend." This rule also applies to the current situation. We should understand that the thinking process of every individual is different. Every person perceives the world in a different manner, and to understand an individual, one has to enter into his/her world, interests, thinking process, etc.

> *"Study of successful people has shown over and over again that they have a great talent for creating rapport. Those who are flexible can affect large number of people whether as a teacher, a businessman or a world leader."*
>
> **—From Unlimited Power by Anthony Robbins.**

4. Life Partner

Life can be broadly divided into three parts—childhood, adult life (before marriage), married life. The period of being married remains for a longer period, thus requires equal attention as that of family life. Your life partner is like the wheel without which the cart cannot move. At the same time, it is this relationship that is the most difficult and complicated to handle. Those who can manage this boundary well, lead a very successful life. The basic thing is to understand the importance of the relationship.

It may be noted that this relationship has existed on earth from times immemorial with purity, serenity and strength. Despite of all odds, it survives. Even in foreign countries where divorce rates are high, they prefer long-lasting relationships. The basic aim is to keep family ties intact and integrated, and lead a harmonious life. Some of the well-proven techniques for this are as under:

(a) Trust

Mutual trust is the foundation for building a strong married life. Whether a building can collapse due to a light gust of wind or by a tornado, depends solely on the strength of the foundation. The building of marriage requires strength, or in other words trust, for longevity of the relationship. This of course depends on both the partners. As a matter of fact, any long-lasting relationship survives on mutual trust. So develop mutual trust at home with your partner.

(b) Maturity

Maturity not only helps in overcoming many difficulties but also takes care of hurried unwanted collapse. It has been observed that married life becomes more stable day by day due to maturity. Certain words used by the partner could have rattled him/her five years ago, but may not be disturbing now. Maturity can take care of this problem. At the beginning of married life, husband and wife are two entities, but they gradually start fusing into one through mutual understanding and maturity. It is an ideal situation and no circumstance can disturb or disrupt this bond.

(c) Consultation

Consultation is better than confrontation. Any decision in the house should be taken only after consultation with the life partner. This establishes the importance of your partner. It must be remembered that every person has self-esteem. Some people ostensibly show it while other hides it. This should not be one-sided, and both the parties should be ready to consult each other.

(d) Mutual Approach

One important formula for a successful life is not to be liability on your partner, as far as possible. Every person should carry out his/her responsibility. Both persons must share responsibilities equally in the partnership and avoid dominance of the other. Mutual respect to each other's feelings is necessary for a successful partnership.

(e) Equality Approach

Equality between both partners is as important as trust between them. Before marriage, there may have been difference in status, qualifications, etc. But after marriage homogeneity should be maintained by mixing heterogeneous entities, otherwise one may develop an inferiority complex, which is not a healthy sign of any married life. The fact remains that our society is male dominated and the status of women is generally not equal to that of a man. Especially when the husband is not working and the wife is the earning member, the man could develop an inferiority complex. The situation can get ugly if prolonged. The right thing to do is to be of compromising nature, and generate a feeling of equality, as both partners are equally responsible for maintaining their family.

(f) Caring for Needs

Proper attention should be paid for fulfillment of needs. This is especially so in the context of our country, where most women are housewives and depend solely on their husbands both mentally and physically. A successful life partner understands these needs very well and gratifies them at opportune times in order to avoid any complaint. This again is mutual respect for each other. The negative impact of non-fulfillment of needs is immense and could lead to fragmentation and sometimes even divorce.

5. Parents, In-Laws and Others

After marriage, there is a change in the set up of the home environment. The bride leaves her home and joins an unknown family, while in the bridegroom's house there is a new entrant who will pass her remaining life there. So there is turbulence in the minds of all the members.

The girl feels that her husband must pay maximum attention to her and spend most of the time with her, whereas his parents want their son to provide the same love and time for them as before. The son now becomes the center of all activities.

Nobody is wrong in their place. But the parents must realize that they have to share their time with the new entrant who has to start life afresh in a new environment. At the same time, the young bride too must realize she cannot have as much time with her husband as she desires, because his role as a son has to be fulfilled and he definitely has to look after the needs of his parents and other relations.

On the other hand, the newly wed groom should understand that his wife has come away from a family in which she grew up. He should not insist that she does not do anything for her parents or family. When the man can think and act for the welfare of his family, similarly his wife has the right to think about her paternal family and tend to their needs.

Ponder on these points. The priorities for both families should be identical to avoid any conflict. It is worth mentioning here that conflict is the consequence of different priorities.

The requirement here is to manage this boundary with rationality without disturbing emotional ties. Generally, the man is busy with his job is not able to manage all the fronts at home. An agreement can be reached between both partners to manage all the boundaries with equality, but with the understanding that any imbalance would not disturb the harmony of the home. It should be always remembered that although husband and wife are two human beings, they are actually one entity called the family.

6. Friends and Other Influential Persons

The role of friends and associates cannot be ignored in day-to-day life. They too have to be tackled in an effective manner. It may be noted here that every individual should be given equal importance in life. You never know, when you may have to approach a particular individual for help. So, keep in touch with them on a regular basis.

(a) Call on Them

Prepare a list of such friends and associates and either meet them or call them on phone occasionally. Some ideal occasions are birthdays, marriage anniversaries or any festival. It will give them a feeling of your concern.

(b) Gifts

In metropolis cities, this is a good method to employ. Giving gifts on certain occasions will smother the feelings about each other and an informal relationship begins.

(c) Dinner Party

Find an occasion when you can invite them for a dinner party. It may be your birthday, marriage anniversary or some other important occasion. It gives them pleasure and also helps strengthen your links with them.

7. Neighbors

Man is a social animal. So, social norms are to be followed by individuals. Maintaining good relations with your neighbors is part of boundary management of an individual. If relations with your neighbors are not good, then you may not have a peaceful life. Techniques for this are to be developed by the individual. Some of them are as follows:

(a) Offer Help: Occasionally, ask you neighbor, if you can be of use to him in any form. If yes, try to do that. It indicates your concern about him and he will also try to reciprocate the same.

(b) Appreciate: Appreciation is a quality which brings people closer to each other. It is ideal to appreciate individuals in front of others. This will help to speedily disseminate your appreciation of any individual. Similarly, good actions or qualities of neighbors need to be appreciated in public so that this reaches them through a third party, and its positive impact will reinforce the relationship.

To conclude, it is most important is to have the skill for human engineering, or develop dexterity in handling human beings in order to manage "Self-Boundaries". It is only this which works, irrespective of any qualification or merit you possess.

❑

15

Conflicts Management

"You can't solve a problem on the same level in which it is created.

You have to rise above it to the next level."

– Albert Einstein

Life is like a rainbow with different colors. It is this which makes it more exciting. Think of a situation if life does not have any color. Then perhaps we would have been dull and dreary. It is my personal opinion that sorrows make us enjoy happiness. A person is lucky to have good days in life, because if he falls into bad times later, then he can derive happiness from the memories of the good days.

One of the colors of life is "conflict" which is faced by every human being in various degrees. Conflict is inevitable in a world as complex as ours and dealing with conflict is an art. This conflict is again related to human management, that is, how you manage with different human beings. If we fail to do so, we may be surmounted by problems. A specific skill is required to manage conflict in day-to-day life. Let us deliberate on the following:

1. What is Conflict?

It is basically the difference of two or more persons in mental status or perceptions on some issue. Living with conflict is very much like having a rhinoceros in your living room. It is irritating. It is risky. It takes attention away from more important things and it can be repulsive. Conflict is a reality that is faced by us daily, in office between subordinates and the boss, within departments, at home between husband and wife, grown up children and parents, mother-in-law and daughter-in-law, etc. Whenever your needs or values come into opposition with those of others, it can result in conflict.

Some conflicts are minor and relatively easy to handle. Others are of greater magnitude and require the use of strategies and skills if they are to be resolved successfully. Some conflicts cannot be resolved, but can be managed. Sometimes conflicts are necessary to resolve problems. Simply agreeing to everything your senior says is also not healthy. But the conflict needs to be resolved effectively before it becomes cancerous.

2. Reasons for Conflict

(a) Imbalance in Different Roles

As you are aware, we have to perform different roles throughout our life. These include the role of a boss, subordinate, father/mother, brother/sister, husband/wife, friend, colleague, etc. As soon as there is imbalance in the performance of different roles, conflicts rise. Thus, it is necessary to balance out the roles. It is observed that most workaholic officers are themselves responsible for ruining their family life. A young married man faces conflict with his wife when he is not able to devote time for the welfare of the family. He might be spending too much time in office, giving more priority for his parents, siblings and other relatives, or undermining his role as a son-in-law. So, it is evident that imbalance of roles is the main cause of conflict.

(b) Difference in Priority

This is another important cause for any conflict. In office you can easily have problems with the sub-ordinates if they are not able to complete the work on time or leave for home without completing the job. This shows that the priority of the two is clearly different. The boss has given weightage to work, whereas for the sub-ordinate the priority is to leave office and do something else. Similarly on the home front too conflicting situations arise in day-to-day life. You accord first priority to work while your life partner thinks that time for self and enjoyment should come first.

(c) Difference in Perception

Most often, we become prey to this phenomenon. Everyone perceives an individual differently as per his/ her understanding, background, experience, etc. Seldom does this perception about the individual change. The behavioral/reaction pattern towards the individual also develops according to this perception. When both persons perceive the same situation differently, it results in conflict. Most professionals face conflict due to different perceptions in their office. A person who is perceived to be good continues to remain in the good books despite committing mistakes, whereas another person who had been originally termed to be inefficient continues to be perceived so, despite his attempts to improve. Hence, it is important for an individual to develop positive perception and there is need to be vigilant.

(d) Communication Gap

This can be termed to be the most probable reason for all conflicts. In fact, most of us are very weak in transmitting and receiving communication. Most of us do not know how to properly communicate what we really want to say, or clearly explain what we have perceived by speaking to another individual. Though facts need to be verified before entering into conflicts, often this is not so. Conflict between two personalities is most of the time caused by negative communication from a third party. These gaps lead to conflicts in every area.

3. Techniques of Conflict Management

Van De Vilert has described the conflict management technique of escalating intervention as a purposeful, systematic operation carried out by an outsider. The technique seeks to increase the frustration experienced by participants during conflicts. Vilert has identified the objective of escalating conflict in groups, many of which indicate an attempt to restore intra-group equality so that the group's communication and effectiveness can be restored. Keeping in view that conflicts need to be resolved, some of the techniques on handling conflict effectively are as under:

(a) Be Pro-active

Most people are presented with a few, if any, formal opportunity to learn the strategies and skills which will allow them to be and feel effective when conflicts arise.

The most important thing is to be pro-active. This requires you to be aware of the values and needs that both you and others have.

The way to do this is to be pro-active. When you first work with someone, be sure to tell him or her about the value this has for you. Discuss possible implications and scenarios. Make a plan to manage it long before it becomes an issue. Ask for an indication that it is clear and acknowledged by both conflicting parties. Decide how the matter will be spoken about as you work together. It does not matter whether you have been working with someone for a while and this has become a major issue. Take the initiative to name, claim and tame the controversy as fast as possible. Focus on 'People Skills for Sustainable Success' to work with individuals and organizations to improve relationships, build and strengthen teams, and manage conflict, anger, and difficult people.

(b) Win-Win Approach

This is the most practical approach nowadays to manage conflicts, for the very fact that you may, in the bargain, lose your identity, your perception, or your views on the issue. A glaring example is the Indo-Pak conflict on Kashmir where both parties are sticking to their position and a positive solution is yet to take place. It is best to adopt a win-win approach, where both parties have something to gain and the conflict gets resolved. In this approach, the need is to respect each other's point of view and each party has equal positioning. This approach is very useful in resolving conflicts.

(c) Emotional Literacy

There may not be any specific course in our educational curriculum on this, but it is still very important to know about your emotional balance, so as to avoid or deal with conflicting situations. It is also good to impart this knowledge to your children so that they are prepared to take challenges in life and deal with conflicts effectively. In fact, it is very important to develop the skill to resist impulses. The cause of many conflicts is impulsive action to a specific situation.

(d) Remain Calm

Although sometimes it becomes difficult, the best thing to do is to stay calm when conflicts arise. If this is not possible, then slowly breathe in and out five times. This may help to avoid conflicts, as the exercise tends to calm you down. I may also help to avoid conflicts and pave the way for constructive discussions for resolving the issue.

(e) Listen and Communicate Carefully

Conflicting situations arise mostly due to misunderstanding with the other party. Thus, it is pertinent to listen to the subject carefully rather than jump to conclusions or attempt to overpower the aggressor of the conflict. Turn to active listening instead of passive listening. Show interest in the subject. At the same time, communicate your point of view in clear terms. One of the best techniques is to find out from the other party if they have understood the intent of what you said. This will confirm the purpose of your communication. Similarly, when someone is talking to you, before terminating the communication, reconfirm whether what you have understood from the communication is as per their intent. In both cases, the communication should be clear and complete. For example, if you want to communicate to somebody you intend to visit him/her there can be two situations – a clear communication and an unclear one.

(i) Unclear Communication

"I will come to your place tomorrow." Here there is no mention of time, the number of persons who intend to go, where they would partake in any meal, etc.

(ii) Clear and Complete Communication

"I will come to your place tomorrow at 9 p.m. for dinner with my wife and two children."

(f) Don't Argue

Arguments lead to conflict, thus it best to avoid them as far as possible. For an inexperienced person, the first reaction to a conflict is to go on the offensive, while the contrary behavior is needed at that time. Conflict is caused by difference of tolerance limits. Usually, before indulging into arguments we forget to gauge the limit of tolerance of the other person, and as soon as tolerance limits are crossed, arguments take place.

(g) Balance Roles

As mentioned above, we have to perform different roles day in and day out. So, it is very important to understand the roles played at different times and try to balance them out. Excessive performance of one role with another may raise conflict. Thus, clear vigil is to be kept while performing each role, and as soon as imbalance is noted, corrective action should be taken.

(h) Synchronize Priorities

This is a most important tool in handling any conflict. It is best if the priorities of individuals match, as otherwise it may cause conflict. Understand each other and match the priorities. Do not let egos play a role. Think deeply and resolve the conflict. If sub-ordinates synchronize their priorities with the boss, if husband and wife synchronize their priorities, then we will find no conflict in daily life.

(i) Sacrifice

Last but not least, if you can develop sacrificing tendencies, then conflicts cannot touch you as an individual, society or nation. It is to be seen whether it is possible to make it a habit or it turns out to be just philanthropic. But still it is worth trying.

In the epic Mahabharata, Yudhishtra sacrificed his kingdom to his cousin Duryodhana. Yudhishtra is revered and respected till this day for this sacrifice. Taking another example from the Ramayana, Lord Rama's sacrifice by proceeding on exile to satisfy his step mother Kaikeyi's wishes, helped to stop any immediate conflict. Rama is worshipped even today for this sacrifice.

Some conflicts can be resolved, based on the approaches written above. But basically, panaceas to conflict are to be discovered by the individuals themselves. Let us try to be conflict free and live this life with happiness and peace.

When (he) was asked from whom he learned goodness, he replied, from those without goodness, because what seemed unbecoming in them I avoid doing my self.

– Sufi Maser

❑

16

Project Management Techniques

Life is the duration between time of birth and death. However, the active life of an adult is taken to be from 30 to 65 years of age (around 35 years). This is the duration when the performance of the individual is rated in terms of his/her active life. In a practical sense, i.e. keeping in view the materialistic society—a successful life is benchmarked as under:

1. Good professional life
2. Sound financial position
3. Good and quality education for children
4. Proper settling of children (job/career, etc.)
5. Sound health of both the partners

And last but not least, the need as per Maslow Theory of Needs

6. Social recognition.

Ideally, all the above six points have equal weightage. It may vary from individual to individual, but this variation is normally not much. Absolute 100 per cent is achievable by the age of 65 years. It is a fact that only certain fortunate persons achieve satisfaction in the range of 80 to 100 per cent. Most people repent some actions taken during their life's sojourn, and on introspection they find that certain decisions were not correct. But nothing can be done to undo these wrong decisions.

Keeping the anticipated fallouts in life, let us take some corrective steps, wherever we are now in the journey of life.

Let's assume life is a project, and we need to manage this project (life) within a defined time, cost and quality.

Some techniques for managing the project are as under:

1. Identification of project manager and his team
2. Regularly monitoring of time and cost
3. Weekly review of progress and identification of constraints
4. Monthly review at management level
5. Generation of various reports for review by the management.

If the techniques are translated in terms of life—it will look like this:

1. Identification of Project Manager and His Team

In this case you are the project manager, and your family members including your spouse and children are the core members. Other family members also form part of your team.

The main responsibility of managing the life project is on you, as you are primarily responsible for any act good or bad. Thus, it is necessary to be prepared for the job. The first requirement for the job is to inculcate the qualities of a project manager.

Former President of India, Dr. A.P.J. Abdul Kalam once said:

"It is essential for a project manager to learn to live with uncertainties and ambiguities. A quotation from General George Patton was given as a counterpoint to this myth – that a good plan violently executed right now, is far better than a perfect executed plan. In my opinion, a project leader should always work with proven technology in most of the systems as far as possible, and experiment only from multiple resources. We learned the hard way that the biggest problem of project management is to achieve a regular and efficient interfacing between the different individuals and work centers. Hard work can be set at naught in the absence of proper coordination."

From the above, it is clear that the project manager has to work with uncertainties and ambiguities. Apart from this he should also be sans ego. It is essential to ensure proper coordination between team members, i.e. with spouse, children and other relations. Any deviation may lead to imbalance.

Generally, in the context of life, ego plays a vital role and a lot of infighting is caused by this factor alone. If you understand the affect of ego – life can be managed in a better way. In fact to succeed either at home or at office, ego needs to be kept at its lowest ebb.

So begin with the first step. Assume that life is a project. Consider yourself as project manager and other family members as members of your team.

2. **Time and Cost**

These are two important parameters which need to be monitored regularly. In the project of life, the section on time is not fixed. It is in the hands of the Almighty, and we cannot control that. The only area within our control is how best we can perform and utilize the time for fruitful purposes. In order to utilize time effectively—short and long term plans for our life can be drawn out. For example, a person of 40 years of age can have the following goals as per time frame:

Long-term: I would have my own house by 2015.

Short-term: By the end of the year 2013, I will publish another inspirational book published.

Mini-term: This month, I would achieve weight reduction by three kilograms.

The cost part of life is one of the most crucial issues. In fact, all people work for financial security in the shortest possible time. In the process, some people may even choose unethical means. Nevertheless, this area needs special attention by the project leader, i.e. head of the family. It becomes the duty of the leader to have sufficient funds at times of need.

Let's take an example. You have a long-term target to have a house by 2010. But the problem is finance. You need funds to the order of 40 lakh rupees but have only 10 lakhs at the moment. The remaining amount needs to be arranged. Identify different sources from which the requirement can be met so that you can achieve the target on time. Missing the target will lead to failure.

However, you must keep in mind that whatever decision you make might affect the lives of the whole family. Suppose you intend to take a loan to purchase a house, and this needs to be refunded. Repayments could affect expenditure on luxuries that the family normally enjoys. Hence, before finalizing the loan, it is necessary to discuss it with the project team—which in this case comprises your family members. Identify the critical issues being faced by the family, like children's education, marriage of daughter; construction of the house etc. These need to be addressed till a mutual and satisfactory solution is got.

Higher education of your child is yet another issue that could need advance planning. Sit calmly with your spouse and review your financial position. Plan how you intend to face the situation and plan for the entire period of education, say four years. Your action should be based on your savings. Of course, nowadays there are banks ready to disperse education loans. Find out more on this and see how you can arrange for this if required.

Proper planning will safeguard you at crucial times, because you have taken all pre-emptive steps and you are placed in a comfortable position. Life is like a game of chess where it is required to think at least two steps ahead before taking any action.

When you work as a project team leader in your life, you need to develop a complex view of the success criteria. There are always multiple, often conflicting, expectations from family members. The process of arriving at the success criteria within a team is an intricate and skilled one because there are a too many minute details to be taken care off, although on the surface the team seems to be simply working to achieve the project's goal.

3. Follow Up and Review

We generally tend to discuss with our spouse only about a specific job we have taken up. We seldom discuss the follow up action or its logical conclusion or completion of that job. It is equally important to give a helping hand at chores at home, as you would at official jobs. Attention should be paid while executing these domestic commitments.

Never give up till the job is completed. Make a list of all the jobs at home and work on them till they are completed. The general tendency is to procrastinate over issues related to the home, often this can lead to avoidable losses. For example, Let's suppose your NSC (National Saving Certificate) matures on a particular date, and you are not able to encash it on time. By this delay you suffer loss of interest over the amount due.

It is necessary to review the progress of different issues, not just big projects. This helps to identify the areas of concern, and take timely corrective action. Let us construct a scene where a husband and wife review the activities of the month.

Husband: How is Raman (son) doing in his studies nowadays?

Wife: Not too good. Since your priority is office work and you have no time for him, he is getting out of hand.

Husband: Why? What's happened?

Wife: Look at his marks in English, they are so low.

Husband: What can we do? I am helpless as there is lot of work in office. Why don't we hire an English tutor for Raman?

Wife: Alright. But you must arrange the tutor within a week. I don't want him to continue getting such low marks.

The next day the husband looks for a tutor and the tuition classes start within a week. One month later the father, mother and son are sitting in a room and reviewing the effects of the tuition classes.

Father: Raman how are the tuitions. Do you find them useful?

Son: Yes father. Now I can understand the lessons better. My tutor is helping me to apprehend and improve in the areas I found myself weak earlier.

Father to his wife: What do you think? Is there an improvement now? (Trying to get affirmation)

Wife: Certainly, he has improved. He scored better in the monthly test and he has also started taking an interest in studies.

Other discussions can be on marriage of daughter, annual savings targets, reduction of weight, etc. The scene and the circumstance may change from family to family. But whatever the issue, it needs to be discussed and it is essential that the project manager takes timely corrective action in a structured way.

Open a register for family issues. Log it every day and after completion of the work strike the completed work out. But continue to review incomplete work with other family members every month. At the end of a financial year, prepare a report (balance sheet) of achievements (assets) and pending work, along with a list showing the financial loans (liability). Analyze the reasons for the same, and take appropriate action on it. It would not only help you but also give guidance to children to manage their life in project management style.

So maintain positive thinking to get more happiness, and your life would have more assets than liabilities in any form.

"If I had my life to live over again, I would have made a rule to read some poetry and listen to some music at least once a week."

–Charles Darwin

❑❑❑